"Face the truth, Mia."

Bram's fingers, light as silk, traced the line of
tension along the nape of her neck.

"Deny that you feel something for me, Mia. Go on,
look into my eyes and deny it," he challenged,
his eyes searching hers, causing ripples of panic in
her stomach.

"No." She tried to twist her face away, but his
fingers raked back through her hair and he held
her head tilted up to his.

"Look at me, Mia. Tell me what you see in my eyes.
You think I feel nothing for you?"

The extraordinary blue eyes blazed into hers and she
trembled at the tenderness, the smoldering passion
she saw in their glowing depths. Was it for her . . . ?

Elizabeth Duke says that her main interest and love is writing, although she's awfully fond of traveling, too. She's visited almost every state in her native Australia, and has traveled to New Zealand, the U.S., Canada and Mexico, which leaves her with no shortage of fascinating settings for her romance novels. The author is married and has two children.

Don't miss any of our special offers. Write to us at the following address for information on our newest releases.

Harlequin Reader Service
P.O. Box 1397, Buffalo, NY 14240
Canadian address: P.O. Box 603,
Fort Erie, Ont. L2A 5X3

WILD TEMPTATION
Elizabeth Duke

Harlequin Books

TORONTO • NEW YORK • LONDON
AMSTERDAM • PARIS • SYDNEY • HAMBURG
STOCKHOLM • ATHENS • TOKYO • MILAN
MADRID • WARSAW • BUDAPEST • AUCKLAND

Original hardcover edition published in 1991
by Mills & Boon Limited

ISBN 0-373-03200-5

Harlequin Romance first edition June 1992

WILD TEMPTATION

CHAPTER ONE

MIA idly toyed with the diamond ring on her finger, and wondered how much longer Bram Wild was going to keep her waiting. She could dimly hear the deep drone of a man's voice from the inner office, and assumed that Mr Wild must have another job applicant in there with him. She sighed. If they'd been closeted in there for this long, what hope did *she* have?

Well, if today comes to nothing, she mused with a shrug, it'll save my having to tell Richard about it. He's made it plain he doesn't want me looking for another job, even a temporary one, with the wedding so close. And maybe he's right. Maybe I should be relishing my new-found freedom ... while it lasts.

She started to tap her foot on the patterned carpet. It was just that ... well, the job sounded unusual ... interesting ... a change from anything she had ever done before. And it was only for a couple of months. Just the kind of break she needed before settling down with Richard.

'Over my dead body!' roared the voice from the inner office, the words slicing through the air as if there were no intervening wall.

Mia glanced across at Mrs Loft, the impeccably groomed blonde secretary who sat between her and the door of Bram Wild's office. For a second their eyes met, then both judiciously averted their gaze.

5

Poor applicant, Mia sympathised, and jumped as the phone on Mrs Loft's desk buzzed. She tensed in her chair.

'Oh, hello, Russ. Sorry, but Mr Wild is still on the phone.' The secretary's tone was briskly efficient, though not unfriendly. 'And after that he has an interview... Yes, all right, I'll tell him.'

Mia sank back in her chair. So... Bram Wild didn't have another applicant in there with him at all. He'd been all this time on the phone! She didn't know whether to feel relieved or put out.

Pursing her lips, she tossed a frown in the direction of the firmly closed door of the inner office. Damn the man—didn't he know she was out here waiting? Didn't he care about appointments?

There was a palpable silence now from the inner office. Did that mean he had finally finished his call? Mia flicked a hopeful look in the direction of the secretary's desk, only to have Mrs Loft give an almost imperceptible shake of her smooth blonde head.

Then the silence exploded.

'*You bloody fool!* What the hell do you think I'm paying you for? Fix it, damn it! Fix it, or you can...'

Mrs Loft spoke then, hastily, her crisply apologetic tone muffling the remainder of the tirade.

'Mr Wild doesn't suffer fools gladly, I'm afraid,' she confided, and she was quick to add loyally, 'But if you do your job he is a wonderful boss. Simply wonderful.' Her brown eyes, under her mascaraed lashes, had softened, Mia noted, and she wondered, with faint cynicism, if Mrs Loft, despite the fact that she was married, was as smitten by Bram Wild as all the other women he had reportedly left in his wake over the years.

Thank goodness I'll never be among them, Mia thought, fingering her engagement-ring in heartfelt relief.

She heard another buzz. Bev Loft was quick to respond.

'Yes, Mr Wild? Right away, Mr Wild.' The secretary nodded to Mia. 'You can go in now. Mr Wild is ready for you.'

Mia let her breath out through slightly parted lips as she rose from her chair. Into the lion's den, she thought. He sounds as if he's in a foul temper. Just in the mood for a job interview!

She paused outside his door and swallowed hard. Why hadn't she worn something more sophisticated than this rather colourless shirtmaker dress? Why hadn't she left her hair loose for a change, curling softly, protectively around her face, instead of pulling it back as usual into this confined, unimaginative style, which, though it might have tamed her riotous red-gold hair, only baldly highlighted her face, she realised now, so that her every expression would be glaringly revealed to this foul-tempered man's scrutiny? Why hadn't she...? She stifled a sigh, pushed open the door, and stepped inside.

Bram Wild was sitting at a large mahogany desk in front of sweeping floor-to-ceiling windows, through which Mia caught a glimpse of the Sydney Harbour Bridge. She had a moment to look him over un-observed, because his dark head was bowed over some papers in front of him. Her application form? Or perhaps the letter from the agency? She felt a stab of irritation that he was only now perusing them. Couldn't he have read all that before calling her in?

His dark hair caught the rays of the afternoon sun, and she could see glinting strands of silver among the dense black. It was surprisingly rumpled, as if he hadn't bothered to comb it, or—recalling his fury of a few moments ago—perhaps he had been angrily running his fingers through it. It curled over his ears and over the collar of his neat striped shirt in a way that suggested he was in need of a haircut. Richard, she mused, would never let his hair get into this state—he wouldn't consider it good for business to look scruffy. But perhaps once you were a top business tycoon like Bram Wild you didn't have to worry about neatness any more.

She couldn't see much of his face, with his head bowed the way it was, but the glimpse she had showed a healthy tan. Which would have been acquired naturally, from the sun, she fancied, because Bram Wild had a reputation for playing as hard as he worked. And Sydney was a great playground if you were that way inclined.

One of his shirt-sleeves was partially rolled up, and his right hand, she noticed with some surprise, was set in plaster. Had that happened when he——?

'Well, Miss James, have you looked your fill?'

She jumped guiltily. And then she frowned. He still hadn't even bothered to look up! She took an aggressive step forward, gritting her teeth. What did the man expect her to do while he was taking his time about acknowledging her presence? Twiddle her thumbs and gaze vacuously out of the window?

'I understood you were ready to see me,' she said in what her mother would have called her 'dangerously quiet' voice. She had a naturally low, well-modulated voice, which she rarely raised, even when she was angry. At such moments it was more likely to become a menacing whisper.

At the sound of her voice Bram Wild's head jerked back. Their eyes clashed momentarily, hers cool and grey-green, locking with his piercing blue, and for a brief, jolting second she saw something in their intense depths that puzzled her. A flicker of what looked like... pain. As if in that brief second his emotions had been brutally stripped bare. And then it was gone, to be replaced by a look of such withering contempt that she wondered if it had ever been there at all.

Was it something he had been reading that had put the look there? Or was it something about *her*?

His eyes dwelt on her face for rather longer than was comfortable, then flicked coldly, almost insolently down her slim body. He made no move to get up, or to put her at ease. His heavy winged eyebrows—devil's eyebrows, she thought them—had drawn together and his lips had tightened to a hard, uncompromising line. Was he trying to cover up that fleeting moment of exposure a few seconds ago, seeing it as a weakness and trying to convince her it had never happened? Or was he always as aggressive as this with interviewees? With everyone? She had already heard what he could be like with anyone foolhardy enough to cross him. Formidable!

'I'm not an easy man to work for,' he barked at her. 'If working under pressure or getting bawled out is going to worry you you'd better leave right now.'

A quiver ran through her, but she stood her ground. She was recalling Mrs Loft's words. 'If you do your job he is a wonderful boss. Simply wonderful.'

'You're trying to talk yourself out of a driver, Mr Wild?' she asked coolly. The undisguised contempt in his eyes was puzzling her as much as that revealing look a second earlier, but perhaps she ought to make allowances for him. Obviously he wasn't himself right now. He had lost his driving licence for two months, and he obviously had a broken hand as well. That must be maddeningly frustrating for a man as high-powered, professionally and in his private life, as Bram Wild was reputed to be.

She had the satisfaction of seeing him waver. Without comment, he rose belatedly from his chair, but he made no move to offer her his hand. Not that he very well could, with it encased in plaster! Briefly, she let her gaze flicker over him, taking in the striped designer shirt with its crisp white collar, the patterned blue silk tie, the well-cut grey trousers. He wore his clothes well, with an animal grace that suggested he would look well in any-thing he wore, even in ragged shorts, if he possessed such things. He was tall—to meet him eye to eye she would always have to look up at him—and there was power in the breadth of his shoulders and a look of coiled-up energy in the lithe, athletic frame.

Without comment, he raised his good left hand and waved her into one of the deep leather armchairs facing his desk, sitting down again as she did.

When he spoke again the contempt in his eyes had faded somewhat. But his tone was still aggressive.

'Why would a young girl like you—a highly talented secretary, by all accounts—want to turn chauffeur for two months?'

His eyes narrowed as he uttered the words, and she saw his mouth twist slightly. Seeing it, her own eyes flashed sudden fire. He didn't think—he wasn't afraid...? She took a swift, indignant breath and swal-lowed hard, determined to stay calm. She supposed she couldn't blame him for being suspicious. Being the super-rich, super-eligible, and not unattractive bachelor that he was, he must have these fears all the time, poor guy—fears that every woman in his orbit was after him. Well, not *this* lady! Mia deliberately raised her left hand to brush an imaginary hair from her cheek, allowing her diamond ring to glint in the afternoon sunlight.

'I take it the ring means you're engaged to be married?' There was no softening in his tone, but it held a faintly puzzled inflection. 'You have set a date for your wedding?'

'We plan to get married three months from now.' Which, if she landed this job, wouldn't give her much spare time to prepare for it. She felt a swift stab of guilt. What would Richard say to that? What would his mother? Her own mother? Why was she so anxious to find a temporary job, anyway? So that she wouldn't have to think about the wedding?

The thought made her catch her breath.

'Don't you need time to prepare for these things?' Now there was marked derision in his tone. Obviously 'these things'—weddings, marriage, a lifetime's commitment to one person—didn't feature in his own thinking—or plans.

She answered with a shrug. 'My fiancé's mother has offered to have the wedding reception at her home. We'll be married in her garden. It's not going to be——'

He cut in, rapping another question at her. 'I understand you're not employed at the moment.' Her wedding details were obviously of no interest to him.

'That's...correct. My long-time boss retired recently and I decided to resign rather than start working for one of the other divisional heads so close to my...wedding. My fiancé doesn't want me to work after we're married,' she explained, adding in a rush, 'he's anxious to start a family as soon as we can. He was an only child, you see, and——'

'Yes, well, let's not go into your fiancé's family tree. So you could start straight away, could you? Working for me, I mean, not having babies!'

Was he actually making a joke? She glanced quickly into his face, but could read nothing from it.

'Well, yes...I suppose I could.' Great heaven, was he actually thinking of offering her the job?

'You hold a current driving licence?'

'Yes.'

'Any driving convictions?'

'None.' Unlike you, she thought, quickly masking the scorn that sprang to her eyes. Did she want this job or didn't she?

'How do you assess yourself as a driver? In traffic? At night? Coping with emergencies?' He shot out the questions like bullets.

She lifted her chin. 'I'm a good driver,' she said steadily. 'I don't get frustrated in heavy traffic. And I don't panic. I enjoy driving. And I have never been involved in an accident.'

'How commendable. Now you realise it's not only a driver I want for the next couple of months? I'm looking for a temporary personal assistant as well. Someone with secretarial skills. In particular, shorthand and accurate note-taking. Someone I can trust implicitly.'

'The agency explained that.'

'You come highly recommended...considering that,' he paused to consult the sheet of paper in front of him, 'you are only twenty-two years old.' A brooding note had crept into his voice, as if her age might after all be a stumbling block. He, Mia imagined, would be somewhere in his mid to late thirties. Perhaps he was looking for someone older, more mature than her, more worldly-wise...

While he was still glancing down, she seized the chance to study his face more closely.

An arresting face, she had to admit. Not handsome, exactly. Ruggedly male, she decided, rather than handsome. Aggressive jaw, firm mouth, deep lines carved in the bronzed cheeks, a hint of danger in the lift of his devil's eyebrows. A strong face—a face exuding vitality, intelligence, arrogance, authority, perhaps even humour on rare occasions... all overlaid with a lusty animal magnetism.

As he looked up again, catching her by surprise, she knew, with a faint jolt, that it was those compelling blue eyes of his that were his most powerful asset. They would draw attention—especially female attention—wherever he went.

And, by all reports, he'd had more than his fair share of that! She recalled what her old school-friend Joy, at the secretarial agency, had said about him, and it was all she could do not to curl her lip in open disdain.

'Women are forever chasing after him... Well, let's face it, Mia, he'd be quite a catch. But he doesn't seem to want to be caught—he's notorious for loving 'em and leaving 'em. Just as well you have Richard to protect you, darling. Having him in the background might make you less susceptible to the potent Wild charm.'

To which Mia had been quick to retort, 'Don't worry, his type leave me cold. I won't need Richard's protection.'

But now, suddenly, as their eyes clashed, Mia was glad of the ring on her finger. Need it or not, it gave her an added sense of security.

He was looking at her oddly, she realised, and she hastily composed her features, hoping she hadn't revealed her thoughts too plainly.

When he spoke again his voice was curt, his eyes cold, with that same insolence in them that had been visible before, as if he had indeed read her thoughts and wanted her to know she had nothing to fear from him!

'I'm looking for someone with a bit of intelligence— a shrewd listener, who can organise her thoughts as quickly and efficiently as she can take notes...someone who will generally be my right hand for the next couple of months, both inside and outside the office. Someone discreet, punctual, and absolutely trustworthy,' he added decisively. His brow shot up enquiringly, and, with a faint gulp, she nodded.

'And——' he cast a baleful look down at his plaster cast '—someone strong enough to help carry bags and satchels when necessary...' He ran a dubious look over her slight frame. 'There'll be some travel involved. To various parts of the state, and occasionally inter-state as well...a day here, a couple of days there. Would your fiancé object to that?'

He would, no doubt, but if it was her job...just a temporary job...

'If that was part of my job, of course he wouldn't,' she asserted, hoping Richard wouldn't make a liar of her. No, of course he wouldn't, she thought loyally. Richard was too gentle a man to kick up a fuss over anything, and, anyway, he wasn't the possessive type— he was always too absorbed in his own interests to put restraints on her.

'Good.' She saw no softening of the rigid features. 'And lugging around bags or heavy briefcases poses no problem?'

She met his piercing gaze with an effort, conscious that her heart was beating a low tattoo in her chest. In all truth, she hadn't expected her interview to get this far. She had had no experience as a chauffeur, or with one-handed bosses, and from the moment she had stepped into Bram Wild's plush office she had been wondering what quirk of madness had prompted her to apply for a job like this over a straight secretarial position, which, with her qualifications, she would have had no difficulty finding. And yet here she was, here *they* were, discussing such minute details as travel baggage... She swallowed before answering.

'I'm much stronger than I look,' she heard herself assuring him. 'I'm very fit.'

That seemed to divert him, for some reason. 'Are you indeed? What do you do? Jog? Play sport?'

'I go to an aerobics class a couple of times a week. That's... about it.'

He gave a snort. 'No outdoor sports? Tennis? Swimming? Surfing? Sailing?'

She shook her head. 'Not... on a regular basis.'

'Then what do you do at weekends, for heaven's sake?'

She bit her lip. Her weekends would sound abysmally dull to a man like Bram Wild. Going to the market, cleaning the flat, visiting her mother, perhaps taking her mother for a Sunday drive, playing the piano for Richard, either at her mother's place or at his unit, so that he could practise his songs for the choir, traipsing around junk shops with him...

'Not an awful lot,' she admitted, her tone unconsciously rueful.

'Ever sailed a boat? You or your fiancé?'

'Never, I'm afraid.'

'Pity.'

At the curt response, comprehension dawned in her eyes. She had read somewhere that Bram Wild was a keen sailor. At the moment, with his hand in plaster,

she guessed he must be finding it difficult—impossible—to handle a boat.

She blew out her breath in a sigh. Yes, it *was* a pity
neither of them could sail a boat. Richard didn't like
sailing. In fact, he detested sport of any kind. When he
wasn't working at the office, or doing extra accountancy
work at home, he would have his head buried in his
stamps or his coins or his antique catalogues. He was a
great collector. And when he wasn't working or collecting he would be rehearsing his singing or going off
to choir practice. There wasn't much time left over for
anything else. There was barely enough time for *her*. If
she didn't play the piano for him, or tag along on his
collecting jaunts, she would hardly ever see him!

'I've always wanted to learn how to sail,' she surprised herself by blurting out.

Bram Wild gave her a quick, penetrating look, and
she saw a glint of silver in the blue. Had her admission
amused him? 'Well, now, have you indeed?'

For a moment longer his eyes held hers, and Mia re-
assessed the look in them. It was more calculating, it
seemed to her now, than amused. Though why... She
sighed, defeated. Whatever the look meant, she very
much doubted there would be any humour in it. Bram
Wild hid his feelings, his human side—if he had one—
almost frighteningly well. Apart from that one fleeting
glimpse earlier, which he obviously regretted.

'We'll have to see what we can do...' He was stroking
his chin now with his good hand, and she found her eyes
riveted to his long supple fingers, to the sprinkling of
fine dark hairs sprouting from his tanned skin. Sensitive, well-shaped hands, she thought idly. Strong, but

with the promise of gentleness too... Gentleness? In
Bram Wild? That seemed unlikely! She swiftly averted
her gaze.

'I'm not entirely useless,' he mused aloud, 'despite
this damned impediment.' He gave his plaster cast an
impatient tap with the hand Mia had been examining
only a second earlier, and for some reason she felt a flow
of warmth to her cheeks.

'If you take this job, you realise it will mean living in
for the duration?' His tone was abrupt again, business-
like. 'You would have your own fully self-contained
apartment upstairs, let me hasten to assure you, with its
own private access, if you wish to use it, from outside.
Mrs Tibbits, my housekeeper, also lives in. As does my
gardener-cum-security man, Alf Jennings, who has
rooms under the house. So you will be well chaperoned,
if such things bother you. Now... would that pose any
problems?'

Her pulse skittered. 'Living in, you mean?' Did he
think she was already living with Richard? That Richard
might kick up a fuss if she moved out for the next two
months? She tilted her chin. 'No problem,' she assured
him. 'My flat-mate, Diana——' she stressed her friend's
name '—is expecting her sister down from Queensland
at the weekend. I'm sure they'd both welcome some time
to themselves.'

'You would be free to have... visitors, naturally,' he
said impassively. Was he still thinking of Richard?
Letting her know that they wouldn't be completely cut
off from each other? 'When I don't need you, that is.'

She gulped, twisting her slender white hands in her
lap. In other words, she would be at Bram Wild's beck
and call, day and night! And poor Richard would have
to be slotted into those times when her employer didn't

need her! Well, Mia James, you knew about all this when you applied for the job. You're either in it to the hilt or you're out. No half-measures.

'I understand,' she said, and was aware of a strange pulsing excitement mounting inside her. It was a crazy, impetuous thing she was doing—or so her mother and Richard would tell her. They would never understand. They would try to talk her out of it if she gave them half a chance. But when was she ever going to have a chance to be crazy or impetuous again? Hardly as Richard's wife and the mother of his children! *Five*, if he had his way! She wasn't even sure that she was ready to *be* a mother yet. Twenty-two seemed so young, and three months away seemed so...so close!

Her fingers tensed in her lap. Could it be pre-wedding jitters that were giving her these doubts, this feeling of restlessness, this disquieting fear that if she didn't do something right away, something new and radical and different, life—youth, freedom, excitement—would pass her by?

'Could you start straight away? Tomorrow?'

She caught her breath. 'You...don't even want to see how I drive first?'

'You can drive me home from the office in a few minutes. My car is downstairs in the garage. If we both survive that, you're engaged. Where is your own car?'

She heard herself answering in a kind of daze. 'I came here by bus. I thought I mightn't be able to find a——'

He cut in, not interested in her parking problems. 'After you've dropped me off you can drive my car back to wherever you live, pack what you're likely to need, and bring the car back again either tonight or first thing in the morning. If your fiancé wants to see what kind of place you're moving into he's welcome to come with you, of course.' Mia saw mockery in his eyes. And a faint look of...challenge?

She chewed on her lip, wishing she knew exactly what he was thinking, exactly what he expected of her. But she had a fair idea. Knowing she was engaged to Richard, he would be expecting them to want to sleep together...if not every night, at least on some nights. If only he knew!

Her mind snapped back to more practical matters. 'You would trust me to take your car?' she asked, showing her surprise. What sort of car did he drive? she paused to wonder. Something racy, no doubt. A flashy sports model to go with his fast-living image? A Ferrari? A Porsche? A Lamborghini? She wouldn't be surprised, bearing in mind the number of times he had been picked up for speeding. So many times that he had finally lost his licence! How would it feel to drive a car like a Ferrari? A far cry from her sedate little Honda! Unless he intended her to drive him around in one of his more sober company sedans. But he'd said *my* car...'

Bram rose from his chair without so much as a smile, and now his eyes were hard as flint again, devoid even of mockery. The niceties are over, Mia thought wryly.

'We'll go now.' His tone was abrupt, almost aggressive. 'I'll take you down.' As they passed through the outer office he paused for a word with Mrs Loft.

'Miss James is going to drive me home, Bev. Would you tell Russ I've gone? He can ring me at home if he wants me.'

'Yes, Mr Wild.' As Mrs Loft glanced from Bram to Mia, Mia caught a look of surprise in the girl's brown eyes, and wondered at it. Hadn't the secretary expected her to get the job?

Well, for that matter, neither had she.

*   *   *

'You drove well,' Bram said shortly, operating his remote
control to open the huge retractable door of his double
garage. A high stone wall, painted white, concealed his
house from the street.

'Thank you, Mr Wild.' High praise, Mia thought,
hiding an ironic smile as she lightly touched the accel-
erator and brought his shiny grey BMW to a smooth
halt in the exact position he indicated. Though hardly
the sports car she had envisaged, the BMW had been a
dream to drive. Feeling its power out on the motorway,
and the way it had responded to her merest touch, she
could understand how easy it would be to break the speed
limit. Though not, she reflected with faint derision, to
the extent that Bram Wild had done. He, from all reports, had been travelling at some quite ridiculous speed,
and had done it once too often...

'You'd better come in and look the place over,' Bram
invited, his tone more terse than friendly. Looking at
him quickly, Mia wondered if he had just had a bad day,
or whether he was always as curt as this with his
employees. And yet he hadn't sounded particularly curt
with Bev Loft earlier, she recalled. Was it just *new*
employees? Or, she thought resentfully, is it just *me*?

Behind the high wall lay a sight that almost took her
breath away. Sloping down to a harbour frontage was
the most beautiful landscaped garden she had ever seen,
with sweet-smelling roses in profusion, sweeping lawns,
graceful elms and maples tinged with crimson and gold—
even a tumbling waterfall. At a lower level she glimpsed
a tiled swimming-pool and a tennis court, and beyond
that was the sweeping panorama of Sydney Harbour.

Dominating the whole scene was his house...

'It's beautiful!' she exclaimed involuntarily. It was like
something from *Gone with the Wind*, an elegant two-

storeyed colonial-style mansion, painted white, with stately columns and wide porches. But so big, for a man who allegedly lived on his own! 'Did you buy it like this or...?'

His mouth twisted. 'When I bought it it was practically a ruin. And the garden was a mess. I renovated the house, and landscaped the garden, and now it is back to its former glory—or somewhere close to it.'

'It must have taken years!'

He looked down at her, and the look he gave her wiped the enthusiasm from her face. There was such scathing bitterness in the look.

'Time means nothing when you are driven by... powerful urges. Come inside.'

Mia bit her lip as she trotted obediently after him, wondering what those powerful urges had been. The urge to show the world what he, Bram Wild, could do? The urge to pour his money into something lasting—producing at the same time a solid investment for the future? The urge to... create a dream? Somehow she doubted that it would be as simple, as romantic, as the latter.

He pressed a button, and a moment later a woman's voice crackled from the wall-mounted intercom. When he announced himself the panelled front door was opened by a large-boned woman of indeterminate age, with pepper-and-salt hair tied back in a bun.

'My housekeeper, Mrs Tibbits,' Bram said without ceremony. 'Miss James is to be my new assistant and driver, Tibby. Will you show her upstairs while I make some phone calls? Oh, and give her a set of keys, will you?'

At the mention of keys, Mia held out the keys of his car, but he made no move to take them.

'You keep those. You'll need them to drive home to get your things. I have another set if I need them. Let me know when you're back.'

Mia bit her lip as she followed him inside. Had he finished with her for the night?

'Will you be wanting me to drive you anywhere this evening, Mr Wild?' she asked when he didn't enlighten her. They were standing now in a marble-tiled entrance hall, with a sweeping staircase to one side and a magnificent crystal chandelier overhead. A wide central passageway, its white marble-tiled floor gleaming, ran the full length of the house, and sunlight streamed in through the graceful french doors at the far end. The high ceilings and basic white colour scheme gave a feeling of light and spaciousness, and for a bachelor's home—especially a bachelor as tough and aggressive as Bram Wild—it came as something of a surprise.

'No, I'll be dining at home tonight. Eight o'clock, if you want to join me. Mrs Tibbits always prepares far too much for one person. Dress any way you're most comfortable,' he said indifferently. 'I won't be lingering over dinner—I'm expecting some calls, and then I have some reading to catch up on. Please yourself, if you'd rather dine with your fiancé. I won't need you tonight.'

It wasn't the most gracious of invitations, but it surprised her none the less. During the time she was living and working here did he expect her to take her meals with him every evening? Or just until she was settled into her apartment? She would need to bring supplies of food in...

He seemed to sense her dilemma, almost to read her mind. 'It will be easier if we eat together while you're working for me, but if you want to dine in your own rooms at any time, or have friends in, Mrs Tibbits will arrange it. You will find some provisions in your kitchen already—tea, coffee, that sort of thing.'

'Thank you, Mr Wild,' she said dutifully. It seemed he had thought of everything!

CHAPTER TWO

'YOUR fiancé didn't want to spend the evening with you?'

Bram Wild's sardonic tone nettled Mia. 'I didn't see Richard,' she admitted, wishing now that she'd had something to eat back at her flat with Diana, or even gone home to her mother's for dinner, instead of coming back here to dine with Bram Wild. Why *hadn't* she?

'He had already left for choir practice,' she explained in her soft, melodious voice, curbing her irritation. 'I thought I'd come back and get settled in here, and then ring him later this evening. If I may,' she added sweetly.

'Ring away. There's a phone in your room.' He had changed, Mia noticed, into a casual open-necked shirt and hip-hugging jeans, and looked even more aggressively male than he had earlier in the day in the expensive business suit he had worn with such flair. 'No trouble with the car?' he asked, pouring a glass of wine for her with his left hand, and not spilling a drop.

'None at all. It's a pleasure to drive.'

'Good. And your rooms have everything you need?' The sardonic note was still there, she noticed, and she felt vaguely irked by it. Did he expect her to lick his boots with gratitude because he'd given her this job and was allowing her to move into his home for the duration? Or was he just being his usual derisive self? She wondered if she would ever get to really know this man— if he would ever *allow* her to get to know him. Or if she would even want to.

24

She gave him a long cool look. Everything she needed? That was putting it mildly! The rooms she had been given were more like the penthouse suite of a plush five-star hotel, with not one but *two* double bedrooms, each with its own palatial *en suite* bathroom, a spacious lounge-dining-room, and a bright, functional kitchen. She wondered what Bram normally used the rooms for. For installing his succession of mistresses? she mused cynically.

'It's most comfortable,' she said primly. And you needn't think you're going to add me to your tally of conquests, Bram Wild, she swore under her breath.

For the first time she saw a glimmer of real amusement in his eyes, as if he had read her very thoughts. 'I'm glad you approve,' he drawled. 'It's handy having the rooms up there.' *I'll* bet, Mia thought with an inward sneer, only to be surprised at what he said next.

'My sister Hope and her family often use them when they come down to Sydney. They live up in the Blue Mountains. But at the moment they're overseas. And on rare occasions my father and stepmother come down from the country to stay for a day or so. They loathe the city, and only come to town when it's absolutely necessary.'

Well, at least the man has a family, Mia thought in relief. It made him seem more human, somehow.

'Lord, it's been a hell of a day!' Bram reached up with his left hand and raked his long fingers through his hair. He had brushed it, Mia noted, before he'd come in, but now it looked as tumbled as ever. If the gesture was a habit he'd fallen into no wonder his hair always looked so rumpled!

'It must be wonderfully relaxing having a place like this to come home to,' she ventured, hoping that was what he would do now that he was at home—relax, and stop baiting her at every opportunity!

'It's like a holiday every time I walk in the door.'

Mia's breath caught in her throat. She hadn't expected such a revealing answer. Or that his voice could change so suddenly, so dramatically. Devoid for once of its usual abrasiveness, his natural tone was rich and deep and faintly lilting. A mesmerising, deeply attractive voice.

Swallowing, she nodded her understanding. A man as busy as he was, away from home so much—how he must relish having a place like this to come home to! But didn't he get lonely here without a wife, without a family? Or was he satisfied with the women who came and went in his life—women he could beckon or dismiss at will?

As the questions flitted through her head she saw an icy chill enter his eyes, and she shivered. What if he could read minds? Or was it simply that he was regretting that glimpse he had given her a moment ago of his softer, more human side? Of course, to him she was a mere employee... He wouldn't want to get too close.

Mrs Tibbits was a welcome diversion as she bustled in with two bowls of steaming pea soup. They weren't eating this evening in the formal dining-room, Bram having confided to her earlier that he preferred to dine informally when he could, here in the sun-room—a brightly decorated, cosily furnished room adjoining the kitchen. There was a round glass table with charming pale blue chairs, a couple of sofas, a television set, and a telephone. During the day, Mia thought, with the sun streaming in through the full-length windows, it must be delightful in here.

'You saw your flatmate Diana?' Bram asked as Mrs Tibbits disappeared from the room. The chill in his eye,

Mia was thankful to see, was no longer evident, his face now totally impassive.

'Yes, I did, and there's no problem, Mr Wild, about my moving out for a while. Di thinks her sister will probably stay down in Sydney a bit longer now.' Diana had called her new job a 'hoot' and had been all for it, bless her.

'If we're going to dine at the same table now and then, and be in each other's pockets for several weeks, I think we could be on first-name terms ... at least outside the office,' Bram drawled, in a tone that seemed more mocking than friendly. 'You can call me Bram. Your name is Mia, isn't it?'

She nodded. He would have learned that from her application form. As she bowed her head over her soup she wondered what other formalities he would want to dispense with, now that she was staying here under the same roof. No, he wouldn't dare try anything, came the swift afterthought. He hadn't brought her here for any nefarious purpose... He *needed* her. He needed her help, her expertise. He'd be a fool to jeopardise that. Let him try!

'Mia...' He repeated the name idly. 'Unusual name. Italian, isn't it? You don't look Italian. James certainly isn't Italian.'

She hesitated, her spoon suddenly motionless in her hand. 'My father chose the name,' she said stiffly. And then she heard herself explaining tonelessly, 'He liked ... all things Italian.' More, she thought, then he had liked his own family...

'Mia...' He said the name again, eyeing her through half-closed lids. 'The name suits you.'

Mia didn't answer. Her mind was back-pedalling into the past. She must have been about ten years old, she reflected, when she'd learned that the name Mia meant 'mine'. A cruel irony... She hadn't been *his*—her father's—for very long. Two short years. Then goodbye, Mia. She felt a brief flare of bitterness. A bitterness that was still there, after all these years. Of course, it had been kept alive, in a thousand subtle ways, by her mother, who would never forget or forgive.

'Your parents live here in Sydney?' Bram was asking.

Mia eyed him speculatively from beneath her thick lashes. Was he really interested, or merely making conversation? She suspected it was more likely to be the latter, and that if she went into too much detail he would quickly get bored and cut her off.

'My mother does. My... father died when I was sixteen.'

No need to explain that it was her stepfather who had died when she was sixteen. Martin James had been more of a father to her than her real father had ever been. She had taken his name... James. Her real father was still living overseas, as far as she knew, with his second family. The only family he cared about, or acknowledged.

'Brothers? Sisters?'

'A younger brother. Paul.' Computer-mad Paul, her half-brother. 'He's away at school camp at the moment.'

'You have told your mother about your new job?'

Mia flushed. 'Not...yet. It's her bridge night tonight. I'll... ring her later, after I've spoken to Richard.'

Bram's eyes narrowed. 'You seem a trifle apprehensive about that. Didn't your fiancé want you to take this job?'

Her flush deepened. 'He... doesn't even know about it yet. I—I didn't really expect to get it, you see.'

She expected him to take her up on that, but instead he asked roughly, 'You're *afraid* to tell him? You expect him to object? What will you do if he does? Change your mind and leave?'

She set her spoon down with a faint clatter. 'Certainly not. And of course he won't object.'

Bram's face was grim now, his brow drawn, shadowing the intensity of his blue eyes. 'If he does, will you stand up to him? Or will you give in?'

Mia sucked in her breath. So that was what this was all about. Bram wanted to be sure she was here to stay. 'Richard isn't like that,' she assured him. 'He's a very gentle, reasonable man. Even if he doesn't like the idea, he would never force me to leave. Especially not now that I've started.'

'But he might have tried to talk you out of it if you had told him before?'

Mia chewed on her lip, considering. 'Oh, no...I don't really think so. It wouldn't have done him any good,' she amended with a quick smile.

His brow rose. 'So you're not under your fiancé's thumb? You can make decisions on your own and...stick to them?'

Mia looked up at him, puzzled by the intensity in his voice, by the strange brooding look she saw in his eyes. Did he simply want her assurance that she was going to stick the job out? Yes, that must be it. He'd hardly want to start interviewing all over again.

'Of course I can,' she said with a decisive tilt of her chin. 'And I am certainly not under my fiancé's thumb.' The very thought made her smile again, more openly this time, and she saw his face relax slightly, and would have sworn she saw a flicker of surprise in his eyes. Why *surprise*? She felt a flare of resentment. What did he think she was? A weak-willed, spineless puppet, too lacking in spirit to stand up to the man she intended to marry? Well, he would see!

'Would you like to meet him?' she challenged. 'I'll ask him to come over. Tonight,' she added recklessly. And after you've met him and left us, Bram Wild, she added silently, you can wonder for all you're worth whether or not I'm going to invite him to stay the night! You will never know. Not unless you prowl the grounds at night, keeping a watch on who goes in and out. Because, with that external staircase leading directly down into the garden from the balcony outside my suite, no visitor of mine needs to go down the main staircase to get outside!

'Please yourself,' he said indifferently, and no more was said on the subject. Over Mrs Tibbits's excellent casserole of curried lamb with glazed carrots and snowy white rice, Bram gave Mia a brief run-down of his business interests—his wheat farm and huge wheat silos in New South Wales, his flour and starch mills in three Australian states, with others in New Zealand and North America, his huge storage depots, his railway yards, his various offices—the head office Mia had already visited in Sydney, and the branch offices dotted around the country. A huge empire! Mia's head reeled. And Bram Wild had built it all from scratch. No wonder he had a reputation for being a workaholic! And no wonder he played hard and fast—he'd hardly have the time to play any other way!

'Damn!' She heard Bram's muttered curse at the same time as she heard the *clink* of glass hitting glass. Bram, attempting to pour some more wine into her glass with his left hand, had knocked the bottle against the rim of her glass.

'Have I chipped it?' he growled. 'Afraid I haven't completely mastered the art of using my left hand yet.' He glared at his plaster cast. Only his thumb was free, and the tips of his fingers—not enough to be of much help to him, though Mia had noticed that he did try to make use of them whenever he could. But it must be difficult, and she could understand his feeling frustrated at times.

She looked down at her glass. 'No, it's fine,' she said, examining it. 'But please, no more wine,' she begged.

She saw his lip curl. 'You want to keep a clear head for when you attempt to justify your new job to your lover?' he drawled, his eyes taunting her.

'I don't need to justify this job, and he's not my——' Mia clamped her lips shut, her face flaming. Damn, she thought, furious with herself, now what have I done? Now he'll *know*.

'Not your...lover?' Sudden amusement danced in Bram's blue eyes. But in an instant it was gone, to be overtaken by a harder, more cynical expression, deepening the lines in his cheeks. 'I didn't think such old-fashioned prudery still existed.' It was said almost with a sneer.

Because she was still angry with herself for letting the truth slip out she vented her anger on him, quite forgetting for a second that he was her new employer. 'Oh, what would a man like you know about such things as morals and old-fashioned values?' she burst out. 'A man with the enormous experience you've had with...with easier, more *worldly* women!'

At the leap of quick rage in Bram's eyes, she raised a slender white hand to her throat.

'Oh, so you think you know all about me, do you?' he rasped. 'Precisely what *do* you know about my private

life, young lady? And where did you dredge it out from?
I certainly don't go around shouting about it. I refuse
to give personal interviews, and I never allow photographs, unless they're to do with my business, so any
trash you've read or heard about me *or my women* has
not come from me...it's all pure, vicious speculation!'

Mia drew back, surprised that he would get so heated
about a bit of harmless gossip. He must know that a
man in his position would be fair game. A bachelor, a
wealthy businessman, a man with a magnificent
harbourside property like this...

'I'm sorry,' she said quietly. Rallying, she added
daringly, injecting a teasing note into her voice, hoping
to defuse the situation, 'You're saying that all those gor-
geous women I've heard about are malicious
fabrications?'

There was a palpable silence, during which he eyed
her narrowly, the changing expressions in his eyes
shadowed, unreadable. And, she suspected, her spirit
wilting a bit, possibly even dangerous.

When he finally spoke she flinched at the withering
contempt in his voice. 'Believe whatever you like! I don't
give a damn. If the way I live my life is such a shock to
your delicate, virtuous sensitivity I'm surprised that you
wanted to come and work for me.'

She drew in a deep breath. 'How you live your life is
entirely your own affair, Mr Wild,' she said, so quietly
that he frowned—whether in anger or because he hadn't
heard her clearly she couldn't be sure. Heedlessly, she
pressed on, tilting her chin. 'You're a bachelor—you're
free to do whatever you like—with whomever you please.
While I'm working for you I'll try not to cramp your
style,' she added rashly.

His hand shot out to clamp down on hers, and Mia cried 'Ouch!' because he had unthinkingly lashed out with his right hand—the hand in the plaster cast.

'Damn...did I hurt you, Mia?' he said in a low growl, jerking it back, away from her.

'No, no, I'm fine.' Mia was staring down at her hand, mesmerised by the fact that his good hand had reached out and was now stroking it. And his touch was gentle, just as she had earlier imagined it could be.

But his tongue was not so gentle. 'So...you'll try not to cramp my style, will you? How bloody righteous you sound! Let me suggest that in future, Mia, you concentrate on the job you have to do, and leave my private life the way I want it—private.'

Profoundly rebuffed, she nodded dutifully. 'Yes, Mr Wild.'

She jumped as he banged the table with his fist—his good one this time. 'For heaven's sake, Mia, do you have to keep on calling me Mr Wild? Don't tell me you're a girl who can't take a scolding?'

She looked up at him. 'No, Bram,' she said at once, and, incredibly, she felt a grin tugging at her lips. Could there possibly be a human side to this ogre? There had to be...somewhere! Not sure yet if Bram had a sense of humour to match hers, she sobered hastily. 'How did you break your hand?' she asked curiously, anxious to change the subject. 'Did you crash your car when you were...' She hesitated, not over-keen to feel the lash of his tongue again.

'When I was picked up for speeding?' He spelt it out, his tone faintly mocking now. At the same time he was eyeing her narrowly, as if he had caught that fleeting grin and was busily digesting it. But he went on without alluding to it. 'I'm afraid it was a bit more colourful than that. I threw a punch at someone.'

Mia bit back a gasp. He certainly looked aggressive enough and tough enough to get into a fight, but for a man of his sophistication, a man in his position... She swallowed, not sure what to say.

'I've shocked you.' Rather than looking penitent, he looked contemptuous, if anything, as if *she*, not he, were the one at fault. 'You are one of those people who believes there is no justification for hitting out in anger—no matter what the provocation?'

'There are better ways to settle an argument,' Mia said tightly.

'Oh, you believe in turning the other cheek, do you?' His tone was scathing. 'How commendable!'

'I believe that words are more effective than force,' Mia said quietly.

'Yes, well, this guy wasn't listening.'

Mia drew in a shallow breath. 'Did he hit you first?' She had been around gentle, reasonable people all her life. She found it hard to understand grown men fighting, in any circumstances.

'I'm sorry to disillusion you, but no, he didn't. Look, let's skip it, shall we? You'll be relieved to know you won't have to suffer the indignity of having to accompany me to court,' he added with heavy sarcasm.

'You mean you paid him off?' Mia caught her breath as she realised what she had said. Oh, no, now she'd done it! Now he would dismiss her on the spot! If he didn't wring her neck first. He looked as if he was severely tempted.

An endless, agonising silence followed. She almost wilted under his fierce gaze, but somehow she managed to keep her chin up and meet him eye to eye.

'I apologise for that,' she said at length.

He glared at her a moment longer, and then suddenly his brow cleared and he actually laughed. *Laughed*! A fulsome gust of laughter which appeared totally free of rancour or resentment.

'Well, you have spunk—I'll say that for you. And I must say I'm surprised.' As her face relaxed, his own immediately darkened, his smile vanishing as if it had never been there, his eyes icy cold, lashing her. 'Just don't expect to get away with it too often,' he warned.

She ran her tongue along her lips. 'No, Mr Wild.'

He jerked back in his chair, throwing up his hands. 'Bloody hell, Mia, do you have to revert to that plaintive "Mr Wild" every time I bark at you?' He waved his plaster cast in front of her nose, glaring at it in distaste. 'I wish I'd told you this had happened during a sailing accident. Or falling down a flight of stairs in a drunken stupor. Would that have been more acceptable to you?'

She bit her lip. 'I'd rather hear the truth from you,' she told him quietly, thinking, If I'm going to be living and working with you for the next two months, Bram Wild, I'd prefer to know what kind of man I'm living and working *with*.

He gave her a black, layered look, and, in the heavy silence that accompanied it, Mia, valiantly meeting his gaze, tried to read some meaning into the look, and gave up, defeated.

'Would you indeed?' he said finally, and there was raking scorn in his voice. 'Well, maybe the story I gave you was the truth, and maybe it wasn't.' And he added tauntingly, 'Maybe I invented it just to get a reaction from you.'

'Why would you want to do that?' she asked, wide-eyed.

'Yes, why would I?' He waved a dismissive hand, and twisted round in his chair. 'Mrs Tibbits!' he bellowed. 'Are we going to get any dessert or not?'

Mia was left wondering just what the truth really was about his broken hand. But it had revealed one thing: Bram Wild was a man of powerful, complex emotions, and explosive passions. One wouldn't want to cross him too often. Not unless one felt strong enough to fight fire with fire. And she, young and inexperienced as she was, sheltered all her life by a gentle, loving family and more recently by a gentle, loving fiancé, hadn't had a whole lot of practice at that.

'You're not serious? You've got yourself another job?' Richard sounded more confused than angry. 'But why, Mia?'

'You know I like to keep busy,' Mia said vaguely.

'I would have thought that the plans for the wedding would have kept you busy enough...'

'Not...really.' Mia swallowed. 'There'll be time after I finish the job to...well, do what has to be done.'

'You're sure this job *is* just temporary? What if he wants you to keep on working for him after he gets his driving licence back?'

'Once he has his licence back and his hand out of plaster, he won't *need* me any more. This is a perfect arrangement, Richard, for both of us.'

'When do you start?' Richard asked gruffly.

Mia took a deep breath. 'Actually, I've already started. This afternoon. I've been home already to collect my things... It's a live-in job, naturally.' She gave him no chance to intervene, rushing on, 'You should see my apartment, Richard. It's lovely. You can come and visit me whenever I'm not working. Why don't you come round now and look it over? Bra—— Mr Wild suggested it, actually.'

'It's a bit late, isn't it? How about tomorrow? I don't have choir practice tomorrow night. I can come over at a more reasonable hour.'

'Richard, it's only just after ten!'

'*Only?* I have to be at the office at seven in the morning for a meeting.'

'Well, I did try to ring you earlier. You usually get home from choir practice around nine. Where were you?'

'I offered to drive Jenny Smith home. Her car's out of action.'

'Oh ... Jenny.' Dumpy, myopic Jenny Smith. A sweet enough girl, Mia acknowledged, but hardly rival material ... Even if I were the jealous type, she thought, which I'm not.

'So you're not coming over?' she asked, and wondered why she didn't feel more strongly about it. She guessed it was because her day had been so long and tiring, physically and emotionally, and she knew she could do with an early night herself.

'Would you mind if we left it until tomorrow?'

'No,' she said frankly. 'But I'm not sure whether I'll be free tomorrow night. It will depend on ... Mr Wild. Better wait until I ring *you*.'

'OK. I'll be here. Goodnight, love.'

'Goodnight, Richard ... dear.'

She woke with a start. What in the world was that thumping sound? It was still the middle of the night!

She realised it was someone knocking on her door. Not the outer door of her apartment, but her *bedroom* door. She jerked herself up on one elbow, blinking into the darkness, still too dazed with sleep to make sense of it. Intruders didn't knock on doors... did they?

'Mia, for goodness' sake, wake up! It's me... Bram.'

Her throat suddenly felt dry. What was Bram Wild doing knocking on her bedroom door in the middle of the night? 'What is it?' she croaked, involuntarily pulling the sheet up to her chin.

'Time to get up. Put on your jeans and a sweater— we're going for a ride.'

She sat bolt upright in bed. 'You want me to drive you somewhere *now*—in the middle of the night?'

'It's not the middle of the night. And yes, I want you to drive me somewhere—to the park. Which is where we'll *ride*. Ride, as in horse. A dawn ride. You'll find it invigorating.'

She lay back with a groan. 'I've never ridden a horse in my life,' she wailed.

'Always a first time. You'll be fine. I'll lead you if necessary.'

'You've got a broken hand! How can *you* handle two horses?'

'I'll manage. Meet you down by the garage in ten minutes.'

She grumbled as she dragged herself out of bed. Well, she had got herself into this... She was at Bram Wild's beck and call now—at any time of the day or night. She might have known that he'd be an early riser. But for him to expect her to join him in his dawn escapades... A dawn *horse*-ride, for heaven's sake! It will be his fault, she thought savagely, if I fall off!

She never would have believed it, but she enjoyed her early-morning ride. A soft golden mist hung over the park as they rode side by side along the tree-lined bridle path. She wasn't scared, because her placid mount was quite obviously used to novice riders, and Bram was right there beside her all the way.

It *was* invigorating, even at a sedate walk. The air at that hour was crisp and snappy-clear, and the old English oaks and ashes were beautiful with the morning sun filtering through their branches, their tips already tinged with the gold of autumn. The shrill warbling and trilling of dozens of different birds broke through the early-morning silence.

'There's a yellow robin,' Bram said suddenly. He was peering up into the branches. 'And...yes, if you look carefully, you'll see a couple of silver-tails...' He identified other birds as they rode along—a blue wren pecking in the grass, a willie wagtail swooping past, a red-browed firetail stalking around the undergrowth. Mia was surprised that this man—this hard-working, hard-playing, hard-talking man—had had the time—had *taken* the time—to make a study of the city's birdlife.

'Perhaps your reputation in regard to *birds* has been misinterpreted,' she quipped, turning boldly to face him.

He turned his head lazily, and, meeting his eye, she saw a whimsical glint in the blue—but in a trice it was gone, the glint turning to ice. 'And maybe you'd be wise to heed the old saying, Mia...where there's smoke, there's usually fire.'

Mia drew in her breath. That sounded suspiciously like a warning, of sorts. A warning? She fingered her throat in confusion. Surely he wasn't intending it in any *personal* way? He had no designs on her, nor she on him. No...he was merely wanting to be frank with her...letting her know that there was some truth behind the rumours about his women, about his dangerous reputation. And yet...there was something about the way he was looking at her, something almost cruel in the curl of his lip...

Suddenly she felt very conscious of her face, parchment-pale and entirely devoid of make-up, and her hair, scraped back into a hasty ponytail. She must look very plain, very unsophisticated, very *unalluring* to this powerfully magnetic man who merely had to click his fingers to have the most desirable women in the country panting for his favours. So why was he looking at her in that... in that...?

She turned away, wishing she had kept his reputation for women out of the conversation. Birds—the feathered variety—were a much safer topic!

'Oh, look—there's another blue wren!' she exclaimed, pointing to a tiny blue bird skipping away through the grass.

'You're a fast learner, Mia,' Bram said approvingly—and she had the distinct impression that there was a double meaning behind the words.

'Got up an appetite yet?' Bram asked as their hour expired and they returned their hired mounts. His eyes, narrow slits of colour under his dark brows, looked bluer than she had ever seen them in the intense morning sunlight, and she felt something catch in her throat.

'I'm starving,' she admitted, letting her gaze slide away from his. Perhaps he had been wise to issue that warning earlier, she thought unsteadily. As she looked down the sun's rays caught the sparkling diamond on her finger, and she thought of Richard. Dear, sweet, unadventurous Richard! She wondered how he would enjoy a dawn ride in the park. He would probably think it was a crazy thing to do. Hadn't she, before Bram had dragged her out?

'Then drive me home,' Bram said imperiously. 'Mrs Tibbits will be waiting with our breakfast.'

'Yes, sir!' she said, turning to him with a smile, unaware of the new sparkle in her eyes, the delicate glow in her cheeks. She wondered why she had never done this kind of thing before. Up at dawn, off to the park for a horse-ride and a taste of fresh early-morning air— to say nothing of an informal lesson in bird-watching. She felt ready for anything!

She felt Bram's eyes on her face, and hastily amended the thought. Well...*almost* anything!

The sun was streaming into the room where they had dined the night before, and the round table, swathed this morning in a bright blue tablecloth, looked deliciously enticing, with fresh orange juice in tall glasses, a basket of fresh croissants and hot bread rolls, jam and marmalade in pots, and a bowl of fresh fruit.

'I hope you're not one of these people who like to chat incessantly over breakfast,' Bram growled as they sat down. 'Because I intend to read the papers.' And, reaching for one of the newspapers which Mrs Tibbits had placed in a neat pile beside his plate, he buried his head and did just that.

Mia took the hint and kept silent, thinking, Well, this is more like the Bram Wild I've come to know...curt, abrasive, rude. I suppose he's regretting those few companionable moments in the park, afraid I might get the idea that he likes me...or, worse, afraid that I might get ideas about *him*!

The very thought made her give an audible snort.

The newspaper rustled ominously, and Bram's frowning face appeared over the top.

'Did you say something, Mia?' His tone was as forbidding as his expression.

She took a deep breath. If he thinks I'm going to quail and shrink back into my box... Surely he can at least be civil at the breakfast table? 'Would you like some help with your croissants?' she asked sweetly.

Bram glared at her. 'I'm perfectly capable, thank you, Mia,' he snarled, and with an impatient sigh threw down his newspaper. He didn't pick it up again, she noticed, until he had finished eating and was sitting back, sipping Mrs Tibbits's hot coffee. But if it was a victory at all it was a hollow one, because when he did speak he chose to talk about Richard.

'I take it your... fiancé didn't come around to visit you last night?' he asked impassively. 'Oh, don't look at me like that, Mia, I haven't been spying on you. Your young man sounds like the type who would come to the front door, that's all—at least the first time. If I'm wrong, and he used the back stairs to your balcony, I apologise,' he said derisively, his blue eyes challenging her.

'No, he didn't come—it was too late,' she said quietly.

'Too late for a goodnight kiss?' His tone was scathing now. 'What kind of wimpish man is this fiancé of yours?'

Mia's face flamed. 'He's a decent, honourable, tender-hearted, *wonderful* man,' she said heatedly, glad that Mrs Tibbits was in the kitchen, out of earshot.

'So he didn't mind you shelving your wedding preparations so that you could come and look after me?'

She wasn't sure she liked the way he worded that, but she was determined to keep her cool. She had the feeling that Bram was baiting her deliberately.

'Richard is a very understanding man,' she said stiffly. 'We agree on everything.' Well, almost everything, she thought, wanting to be honest with herself if not with Bram Wild.

'How boring,' Bram said curtly. 'Well, as long as you're happy with your wimp of a lover—sorry, *admirer*—so be it,' he said insolently. 'Did you get on to your mother?'

Mia nodded mutely. She had rung her mother after she had spoken to Richard, catching her just as she was going to bed after a successful evening at bridge.

'How did she take it?' His eyes taunted her, as if he knew it had been a difficult call.

'My mother...' Mia hesitated. She couldn't in all honesty say her mother had been happy about her new live-in job. She had been appalled!

'She thinks her little girl has gone mad?' Bram suggested, and there was a droll note in his voice now. 'She has heard about my evil reputation, and has warned you to lock your doors at night? You didn't take her advice last night, I notice. I was able to walk straight in.'

'That's because I never for a moment thought it would be necessary,' Mia shot back. 'It will certainly be locked tonight!'

'Oh, hardly necessary. Did I threaten you in any way? Did I venture beyond your bedroom door?' He was laughing at her, Mia realised irritably. The man was a monster! 'I did knock first on your outer door,' he told her, 'but you obviously didn't hear me. I had to come in and knock on your bedroom door or you would still be sleeping like a baby now.'

She grinned then—she couldn't help it. It was probably true!

'Will you be going into the office this morning?' she asked him, prudently changing the subject. She didn't want to think about her mother at the moment, or about the wedding, or even about Richard. She just wanted to

get into the swing of her new job, and try to enjoy it.
If Bram Wild would let her!

'Yes ... for a while. And then we'll be going down to
the Wollongong office for a meeting.'

'Oh.' Wollongong was down along the coast, an hour
or so from Sydney. Bram had a starch mill and an office
there, she recalled his telling her. It should be a pleasant
drive.

Bram reached for his newspaper. 'You'd better go and
get dressed, Mia,' he said without looking up. 'I want
to leave for the office in half an hour.'

She fled, feeling guilty now that she had kept him from
his newspapers. Presumably he would need time to dress
for the office himself, and he hadn't finished reading
them yet. She had a lot to learn about life in the fast
lane, she was beginning to realise.

CHAPTER THREE

BEV LOFT looked up curiously when they walked into the office together. I'll bet she's curious, Mia thought wryly. Bev must know better than most people what a bear of a man her boss can be.

'Morning, Bev.' Bram's tone was brisk. 'Did those papers arrive?'

'Yes, Mr Wild. They're in your office. Along with your mail.'

'Have you opened it for me?'

'Yes, Mr Wild—except for the ones marked private.'

Bram threw up his hands in exasperation. 'For goodness' sake, Bev, how many times do I have to tell you? You can open *all* my mail. It's a damned sight easier for you than it is for me.' As a reminder, he thrust his plaster cast under her nose. 'They'll only be invitations, or requests for money!' A derisive spark sprang to his eyes. 'Love letters are not normally sent to me care of the office!'

As Bev eyed him guardedly from beneath her mascaraed eyelashes he gave a brief explosion of laughter, and barked, 'Introduce Mia around while I look them over. Ten minutes, Mia!' He swung on his heel and vanished into his office, slamming the door behind him.

It felt like the calm after the storm—though the air still rustled with his presence.

'It's just his way,' Bev said, tossing Mia a rueful smile. 'You'll get used to it. Er—how have you coped...so far?'

The way she asked the question made it sound as if to have coped up to this point would be a major achievement!

'So far, so good,' Mia said, smiling back. No need to elaborate. Heaven forbid!

'His bark is worse than his bite,' Bev assured her. 'Not that it can't be pretty frightening at times,' she admitted, 'especially if you've done something to deserve it. He's a great boss, though, so long as you're willing to work hard and be ready to jump when he wants you to jump. If you do, the rewards are...worth it all.'

Rewards? Mia looked at the girl narrowly. What was she implying? That she—that he——?

She didn't want to know! 'Yes, well, hadn't we better——?'

'You're not scared of him already, are you?' Bev looked amused.

'Certainly not.' Mia stood chewing on her lip, a faint frown creasing her brow. She decided to take the bull by the horns. 'Bev...yesterday you looked surprised that I had got the job. May I ask why? Because you think I won't be able to handle it? Working for Mr Wild, I mean. I've worked for demanding bosses before, you know.' Though no one quite like Bram Wild, she added under her breath.

Bev looked a bit hesitant. 'It's not that...' she said, and stopped, shrugging her silk-clad shoulders.

'What, then?'

'Oh, it's just that...well, you're so different from the sort of women he usually wants around him. Working for him, I mean,' she amended hastily as Mia's eyes flashed green sparks.

'Different...in what way?' Mia asked, her voice deceptively soft.

Bev sighed and spread her hands. 'Well...you're so young, for one thing. And you look so...so fresh-faced and sort of fragile—all eyes, slim as a reed, and that flawless white skin. Our boss normally goes for older, grittier, more hardened types. Women who, well, who've been around. Who've seen and done it all. Toughies, like me,' she said, tempering her words with a lop-sided smile.

'I'm tougher than I look,' Mia said, summoning a smile of her own. 'I won't let him walk all over me, I assure you.'

'Good for you. Well, I'd better introduce you to the rest of the team. When he says ten minutes, he means ten minutes.'

Mia nodded, and followed dutifully as Bev led the way in and out of the other offices. The men and women she met went out of their way to be friendly and pleasant, and their ready welcome was warming. Mia had the impression they were a close-knit, hard-working, dedicated team, fiercely loyal to Bram Wild, while not averse to cracking snide but affable jokes about the way he kept their noses to the grindstone.

'Well now, Russ Masters is the only one you haven't met,' Bev said as they headed back to Bram's office. 'He's not in yet. He has an appointment with Mr Wild at ten. You'll probably meet him then. Russ is general manager here—he runs the place when the Mr Wild's not around. Russ has been with Mr Wild right from the start—he goes back to the time when the boss owned only one starch mill.'

She pushed open the door of Bram's office. 'In you go—and good luck,' she whispered.

'Thanks.' Mia sailed past her with a quick smile, wondering fleetingly just why Bram Wild, who apparently preferred older, more hard-nosed women around him, had chosen her—a quiet, unsophisticated twenty-two-year-old—to work for him, knowing full well they would be thrown into close contact in the following weeks.

She decided he couldn't have had too many applicants for the job!

On the dot of ten o'clock a breezy knock made them both glance up from the papers they were working on to see a smiling face peering round the door. 'Good morning,' greeted the newcomer.

'Ah, Russ, come in.' Bram beckoned with his good hand. 'Meet my new driver and right-hand lady, Mia James. Mia—Russ Masters, my general manager. Russ is also the best PR man you can get. He loves organising functions—any kind. Loves attending them too—far more than I do. I couldn't ask for a better GM.'

High praise indeed, from Bram Wild! If he heaped such praise on all his staff, Mia mused, it was no wonder they were so loyal to him.

Russ thrust out his hand. 'Delighted to meet you, Mia.'

'How do you do?' Mia said in her soft voice, smiling as she shook his hand. Russ had a charming, boyish smile and an easy manner—she could see what an asset he must be at business and social functions.

Momentarily, as she met Russ's eye, she caught the same look of surprise she had seen in Bev's. Quickly masked, she noticed.

'We do a lot of entertaining in this business,' Bram remarked from behind, his voice almost amiable for once. 'And Russ thrives on the social side of the business. He's a brilliant organiser. I attend a few functions, of course, but I'm away a lot, and even when I'm here in Sydney I tend to leave that side of the business largely to Russ. I prefer to fill in my time in other ways.'

Like chasing after women, Mia thought caustically,
avoiding his eye.

'Now, Russ...about this Italian venture.' Bram leaned
back in his chair.

'Do you wish me to take notes?' Mia asked uncertainly.

'No need. I just want to toss a few ideas at Russ. You,
Mia, can do something for me.'

'Yes, Mr Wild?'

'I want you to drive back to my place and pick up a
basket that Mrs Tibbits will have waiting for you. I don't
want to waste time stopping for lunch on our way to
Wollongong. We'll eat as we drive. Don't be long,' he
rapped.

'Yes, Mr Wild.' She caught Russ's eye as she turned
for the door. He gave her a quick smile and an encouraging nod. Did he feel she might need a bit of encour-
agement? Maybe he'd seen the way his boss had treated
other tender young female employees in the past, and
felt she might be in need of some moral support.

She sighed faintly as she made her escape, hoping she
hadn't taken on more than she could chew coming to
work for Bram Wild.

'Now it's not going to worry you to eat while you drive,
is it?' Bram's tone was faintly belligerent, defying her
to utter a protest.

'It's only sandwiches. I'm sure I'll manage.' Mia's tone
was dry, her manner cool. That, she had decided, was
the best way to deal with Bram Wild. To remain
unflappable.

It wasn't easy. She could feel his eyes on her, burning
into her profile, causing the tiny hairs on the surface of
her skin to prickle faintly under his scrutiny. 'We'll stop

and stretch our legs when we have our coffee,' he added with less force. 'As long as we're at the mill by two.'

'Yes, Mr Wild.' She already knew that he had a meeting at two, and that she would be required to take notes.

'It's "Bram" outside the office, remember?' He sounded faintly irritated. 'Do you have a problem with that?' He was telling her it was nothing personal, just good sense.

'Of course not ... Bram.'

His gaze was still intent on her face—she could feel it. It made her feel distinctly uncomfortable, but with a supreme effort she managed not to react, concentrating on her driving as she munched the pack of sandwiches he'd handed her. She wasn't going to let the man intimidate her as he must have intimidated other young women in the past. Why *had* he chosen her, of all the women he could have chosen, to come and work for him, if she was the type of girl he normally steered clear of?

Conversation, mercifully, wasn't a problem, because, as soon as they had finished eating their sandwiches and the freshly baked banana cake which Mrs Tibbits had provided as well, Bram picked up the car phone and began making calls. He brought the third one to an abrupt halt, with a sharp, 'Turn left here!' and, as Mia obligingly swung the car around, he explained curtly, 'We'll have coffee at the Mount Bulli look-out. It's worth taking a look.'

He swayed closer as the car turned sharply, and her nostrils quivered at the clean, subtle male smell that clung to him. It was so different from Richard's sharp, spicy aftershave ... elusive, and yet potent. She felt herself colouring, feeling disloyal to Richard at the wayward thought.

When, seconds later, she brought the car to a stop a few steps from the fenced look-out she threw open her door and almost tumbled out, glad for the chance to stretch her legs. Or was it a relief to remove herself from such close proximity to Bram Wild?

The view from the look-out was spectacular. Mia's stunned gaze followed the broad sweep of the Pacific Ocean, skimming along the golden beaches and the scalloped bay, and over the shifting froth of white along the shoreline. The water today, under the pale Wedgwood sky, was a brilliant rippling blue, sparkling with pin-pricks of silver. Off the coast she could see a long dark shadow. A ship of some kind.

Directly below, way, way down, lay a dense jungle of green trees, abuzz with noisy cicadas. The township of Bulli was down there too, and further round to the right was the huge urban sprawl of Wollongong, stretching from the cliffs to the coast, with the smoking chimneys of Port Kembla just visible in the hazy distance.

Mia leaned against the rail, watching two graceful hawks swooping in the heat currents below. She expected Bram's gaze to be following hers, but when she turned round to reach into Mrs Tibbits's basket for the Thermos flask and mugs she realised that he wasn't looking at the view, he was looking at *her*. As their eyes met she felt a tiny current, like an electric shock, run through her. It was the *way* he was looking at her, his eyes half closed, oddly guarded, and yet at the same time seeming to pierce deep into her own, almost as if they were searching for something there.

Shakily, she poured coffee into his mug and handed it to him, then poured her own and began to sip it slowly, eyeing him warily over the brim.

'You have remarkably beautiful eyes, Mia,' he said at length. His tone was matter-of-fact rather than fawning. 'Changeable eyes,' he added musingly. 'Yesterday, in my office, they were as grey as a wintry sea. Today they are quite green; more like the eyes of a cat.'

Mia flicked her tongue along her lips. 'They do seem to change colour,' she said, finding her voice with an effort. 'I...think it depends on what colour I'm wearing at the time, or whether I'm indoors or out in the sun.' She was relieved when his eyes veered away from hers, but her relief was short-lived because now his gaze was roving over her face, her hair. Not that there was any-thing particularly indulgent or admiring about his look, she realised with growing unease. He was frowning, in fact, and there was a dark, brooding expression in his eyes. Nervously she took another sip of her coffee.

'Why do you always wear your hair pulled back like that?' he demanded irritably, disposing of his own coffee in a couple of angry gulps. 'Don't you ever wear it loose?'

She finished her own coffee before she answered. 'It's easier like this,' she said shortly, taking his cup from him as she spoke. Her mother liked her hair confined this way, and so did Richard. It was neat and practical, and attractive without being too showy. Her mother in particular hated seeing it hanging loose and untamed, with curls escaping, tumbling out of control. Anything the least bit out of control smacked of instability in her mother's eyes.

'It's too pretty to tie back like that,' Bram growled, the harshness in his voice making it more a criticism than a compliment. 'You should wear it loose...let it flow...bounce...pick up lights. Right now, with the sunlight on it, it's a whole kaleidoscope of colours—

burnt orange, gold, copper, vermilion...it's like a tropical sunset. You should show it off.'

Mia felt a rush of heat to her cheeks. It was the silver-tongued womaniser talking, she thought faintly, trying not to get carried away.

She was uncomfortably aware that Bram's eyes were still intent on her face, though the shadows playing across his own were hiding whatever expression was smouldering in the intense, hooded depths. No doubt he was secretly laughing at her now, because his extravagant flattery had left her speechless.

'You're not comfortable with compliments, are you, Mia?' he asked after pause, one corner of his mouth curving slightly. 'Doesn't your mother ever rave over her daughter's glorious Titian hair and her lovely changeable eyes?' As he asked the question he reached up with his good hand to feel the texture of her hair with his fingertips, and for a brief moment she had the alarming thought that he was going to tug her hair free from the neat ribbon that was tying it back and let it spill down over her shoulders. But if he had had any such intention he must have thought better of it. It was the lightest of touches, quickly gone. Yet it left her feeling faintly breathless.

'My mother?' She gave a wobbly smile. Her mother raving over her looks? That would be the day! Her mother didn't believe in idle flattery...in elaborate compliments. She was afraid they might turn a young girl's head and give her ideas that would plunge her into all kinds of trouble. And her mother had reason for thinking the way she did. Hadn't she herself once allowed a man's silver tongue to sweep her off her feet...with disastrous results?

'Other qualities are more important to my mother than looks,' she said with a shrug, bending down to replace the cups in the basket. 'Beauty comes from within, she says. You don't flaunt it.'

'And you're a dutiful daughter.' As she straightened, Bram pointedly ran his gaze over her neatly tied-back hair and demure buttoned-up blouse. There was open scorn in his voice now, and a hardness about his mouth that came dangerously close to cruelty. Did something more than the desire to taunt and tease lie behind all this? Mia wondered, her eyes narrowing.

No... She rejected the idea as fanciful, her eyes flaring in swift anger. Plainly the man got his kicks from deriding people like herself—and her mother. What else could she expect from a man like Bram Wild, whose ideas, whose morals, whose whole outlook on life were light-years away from her own!

'A *loving* daughter,' she corrected coldly. 'Nobody's forcing me to be the way I am.'

The way his devil's eyebrows shot up suggested he wasn't so sure about that. Damn him, she thought furiously. But he hadn't finished tormenting her yet. Before she could stop him he caught her left hand and held it up so that the bright rays of the midday sun caught the diamond on her finger.

'Doesn't *he* ever pay you compliments?'

She lifted her chin, trying not to think about the effect his touch was having on her. 'You mean Richard? He...' Richard's face floated into her view. Dear, sweet, dependable Richard... He didn't need to pay her flowery compliments. She knew that he loved her. He wanted to marry her, for heaven's sake! Anyway, compliments weren't his style.

She snatched back her hand. What in the world was she doing, standing here allowing this silver-tongued womaniser—her *employer*—to play with her hand, to touch her hair, to look into her eyes? Was she mad?

'Hadn't we better go?' she asked tensely.

'Running away, Mia?' The half-closed eyes glittered with cynical amusement.

'Certainly not. But if you're to be at the mill by two...'

'I bow to your bidding, Mia,' he said, in such an obsequious tone that she nearly choked. The day this man bowed to anyone's bidding she would do handstands all the way down George Street!

Back in the car, she realised that her knees were shaking. Reaction... Tensely, she wondered why she was getting into such a state over a man who wasn't...Richard.

She sighed in confusion. It was just that Bram Wild was so different from any other man she had ever come across. She had never met a man quite so...so unpredictable, so outrageous, so...unnerving.

She felt a sudden, overwhelming yearning for the solid, safe, uncomplicated presence of Richard. She knew where she was with Richard. She knew what to expect from him, and what to expect of herself. A girl would never feel safe and secure with a man like Bram Wild. She would always be wondering, floundering, uncertain, not knowing where she was from one minute to the next.

'Um...will we be back in town in time for dinner?' she asked tentatively. She would have dinner with Richard, she decided...she would spend the evening with him. She would even play the piano for him if he asked her to!

'I wouldn't count on it,' came the laconic reply. 'My colleagues in Wollongong will probably want me to join them for dinner. Which means you will have to stay there too. Any objection?' She heard the sardonic note in his voice, and carefully refrained from glancing round at him, or showing her disappointment. He's reminding you, Mia, that you are at his beck and call at all times...day or evening. For the next two months you will have to put his needs, his wishes, his *whims* before your own. And before Richard's. There's no point squealing about it. You went into this job with your eyes wide open.

'Of course not,' she said stiffly.

'Anxious to see lover-boy, are we?' His tone was whimsical. 'One night away from him and you're pining for him already. How touching. Why don't you ring him now?' he invited abruptly. 'You can tell him how much you're missing him. Never let it be said that Bram Wild would be so callous as to come between young lovers...*would-be* lovers,' he amended tauntingly. 'Well, go ahead, Mia. I'm sure he'd be delighted to hear from you.'

Mia, her cheeks flaming, drew in a deep breath. 'I...never ring Richard at work. Not...not without a good reason.' Damn! Why was she stammering?

'Isn't love a good enough reason? Won't he be warmed to the cockles of his heart to hear that you're missing him?' She heard the heavy sarcasm in his tone, and wasn't surprised. What would a man like Bram Wild know of love? *Real* love?

She kept her eyes on the road in front, her expression stony. 'He might have a client with him. I'd...I'd rather not.' Richard would hate it if she rang him at the office, just to say hello, just to say 'I'm missing you'. He would be so embarrassed! To say nothing of how she would feel herself, knowing Bram Wild would be listening in, cynical and contemptuous.

'Please yourself.' His tone was dismissive, uncaring. But at the same time she was uneasily aware that his eyes were still boring into her rigid profile, intent, probing... thoughtful. Thinking what, exactly? she wondered, her fingers unconsciously tightening on the wheel. Probably best that she didn't know!

It was late when they returned to Sydney, too late to ring Richard. Was he missing her? she wondered as she slipped between the cool linen sheets. He would have his choir for consolation, she supposed, sighing faintly as she buried her head in her pillow... and his hobbies, and his work. Richard wasn't the type of man to sit around idly and mope. She ought to be glad he wasn't... She *was* glad, she assured herself, rolling over on to her back. She should thank her lucky stars that she had such an understanding, patient, well-adjusted fiancé. A man who wasn't possessive, or jealous, or demanding. There couldn't be too many women as fortunate as she.

Anyway, she would be able to see him tomorrow. Tomorrow was Saturday, and Bram had told her the day was hers, to do with as she pleased. She would ring Richard first thing.

The phone beside her bed shrilled in her ear, waking her. She reached out to switch on her bedside lamp, having drawn all the curtains the night before so that the morning sunlight wouldn't wake her too early. She glanced blearily at her bedside clock as she fumbled for the receiver. Barely six o'clock! Who would be calling her at this hour of the morning? On a Saturday?

'Mia, throw on a robe and come down...now, this minute!'

Bram Wild. She might have guessed. Did he want her to go for another dawn ride before letting her go for the day? But he had told her to throw on a robe, not get dressed. And his voice sounded so...so urgent.

'What's wrong?' she mumbled. 'Is there a fire?'

'In a way. Get down here *now* or you'll be too late. You'll find a towelling robe behind the door of your bathroom. For heaven's sake, Mia, hurry! I'll be on the front terrace.'

'All right...I'm coming.' Heart pounding, blinking the sleep from her eyes, she rolled out of bed and stumbled to the bathroom. She found the towelling robe and dragged it on over her shortie pyjamas, thrusting her bare feet into a pair of slippers. She didn't even pause to check her face or hair in the mirror. Bram had sounded so insistent, and he hadn't exactly *denied* that there was a fire. She had better do as he'd said and *hurry*.

She flew down the stairs, along the wide marbled passageway leading to the front door, which was wide open, she noticed. And that wasn't all. Through the open doors she could see an ominous red glow. Her breath caught in her throat. There *was* a fire. Oh, no, she thought, her heart twisting. Bram can't lose this place! It means so much to him!

She burst out on to the terrace, eyes wide with dismay—only to hurtle straight into Bram Wild's startled arms.

For a second his arms closed around her, enveloping her in their iron strength, and in that brief second his face, hard-boned and deeply tanned, was dangerously close, a heady breath away from hers. His eyes were deep slits of blue under the saturnine brows, and his hair was damp and tousled, as if he hadn't bothered to comb it after taking an early-morning shower. He smelt subtly aromatic and tantalisingly male.

He was already dressed, she noted dimly, shivering faintly in his arms, acutely aware of his plaster cast pressing into her spine, and his other arm, warm and sinewy, burning into her flesh through the towelling robe. Arms, she thought dazedly, that would never let a girl fall, or falter...

Then, with a suddenness that brought a gasp to her lips, he released her, almost pushing her away from him. She gave herself a tiny shake, confused at the reactions running through her and profoundly relieved that he was no longer holding her. And yet mingled with her relief was the oddest sensation that she had just lost the most vibrant contact she had ever experienced in her life.

He gave a soft chuckle, a low seductive sound deep in his throat. 'I told you to hurry down... I didn't mean to alarm you,' he drawled, mockery glinting in his eyes. 'I wanted you to see the sunrise... it's a fantastic sight this morning. No one should miss it.' He turned away rather abruptly as he spoke, and with an effort she pulled her own gaze away and looked beyond him, out over the harbour.

She felt her throat constrict. 'Oh...it's—it's...' Words failed her. She had seen beautiful sunsets before, and occasionally a brilliant sunrise, but never one like this, never one that lit up the sky with such breath-catching radiance, and never, never with this... almost painful intensity of feeling. She felt a faint prickle of tears stinging her eyes as sensations she couldn't define flooded through her.

'You have the look of someone who has just had a sublime experience, Mia.'

She jumped at the sound of his voice, and swallowed hard when she saw that he was facing her again, looking at her through lowered lids, his eyes searching yet guarded, his own expression carefully masked. Was he still laughing at her? There was no hint of it in his voice, but with Bram Wild one could never be sure.

She flushed. Why *was* she so affected by this particular sunrise? Why did she find it so unbearably beautiful that she wanted to cry? Anyone would think she was seeing the sun rising for the first time in her life!

'You don't do this often, do you, Mia?' he asked, his voice, for once, almost gentle.

She looked at him enquiringly. 'Do what?' she asked warily.

'Take the time to stand and drink in the beauties of nature? Don't you and your... don't you and Richard ever have the urge to do this sort of thing together? To share a... sublime experience?'

She looked up at him sharply. Now he *was* laughing at her. If she knew Bram Wild what he had in mind when he spoke of sharing a sublime experience was something far more down to earth than watching a beautiful sunrise together! She felt a thread of heat course along her cheekbones.

'You look very fetching in that towelling robe,' he commented, unperturbed. 'And I like your hair loose and tumbled like that. It makes you look quite...different. Quite...delectable, in fact. You should wear it like that more often.'

Suddenly conscious of the way she must look to him, she let her hand fly instinctively upward. 'I...I didn't even have time to comb it! You...you made it sound so urgent.' Oh dear, he was making her stammer again! He was doing this deliberately...he was trying to put her off balance, for his own private amusement. And he was succeeding, damn him!

'I'd better go and have my shower,' she said, backing away. 'And after that,' she added pointedly, 'I'd like to ring Richard, if I may.'

'You don't need to ask. Oh, and, talking of Richard...' he raised a finger, and she paused in mid-flight '...I have two spare tickets for the theatre tonight. The Ibsen play at the opera house. I'd like you both to come along as my guests. We'll have a bite to eat beforehand at the opera house restaurant.'

Mia stood vacillating in the open doorway. Was this a royal decree? Well, of course it was, she thought impatiently. He will want you to drive him there, and drive him home afterwards. So why not enjoy a night out at the theatre at the same time, with dinner thrown in? It was jolly kind of him to include Richard. It was ages since they had been to the theatre together.

'That's kind of you,' she said politely. 'I'll ask Richard. If he's free I'm sure he'd be delighted...we'll both be delighted...to accept your invitation.'

'You wouldn't come without him?' There was a bantering note in his voice and a challenge in his blue eyes, giving them a strange glitter that caused a tiny shiver to glide down the back of her neck.

'I'm sure he'll come,' she said, avoiding the question. 'I know his choir's not performing tonight, but it's just possible they might have to practise. They've been having extra rehearsals lately because they're busy preparing for their first country tour at Easter.'

'Richard will be away at Easter?' Bram asked languidly.

Mia sucked in her breath. Maybe she shouldn't have told him! He might have felt more inclined to give her some time off over Easter if he had believed that Richard was going to be around, thinking she would want to spend as much time as she could with her fiancé. She nodded mutely, mentally kicking herself.

'Well...' Bram stood stroking his chin '...maybe that's all to the good. Because I'll be wanting you to drive me up to my sister's place in the Blue Mountains for Easter. Good to know I won't be keeping you young...lovers apart.'

She noted the telling pause, and her eyes glinted with suppressed hostility. He never missed an opportunity to rub it in...the fact that she and Richard weren't yet lovers. To him, such outmoded morality was something to be sneered at, ridiculed. A man like Bram Wild wouldn't think twice about tumbling into bed...with any woman! Whether love came into it or not.

Men of his type had no principles, and she despised him for it!

'I'll let you know as soon as I can about tonight,' she said through stiff lips. 'Excuse me.'

'Mrs Tibbits will be serving breakfast out here on the terrace,' he called after her. 'Unless you want to have breakfast with...Richard.'

His mocking tone made her grit her teeth. 'I probably will,' she called back, determined that, wherever she had breakfast this morning, it wouldn't be with Bram Wild. Let him have the weekend papers for company... She certainly didn't want *his*!

CHAPTER FOUR

'RICHARD, I've got the day off. What are you doing now...this morning?'

'Mia! Afraid you've just caught me. I'm on my way over to Dad's to help him put up a new pergola. One of the many things Mum wants done before the wedding. Why didn't you ring me last night? I kept the evening free specially.' Richard was doing his best to sound reasonable, Mia noticed, but he couldn't prevent a faint peevishness from creeping in.

'I had to take Bram to Wollongong, and we didn't get back until late.'

'So...it's "Bram" now.' The peevish note was more marked now.

She took a long breath. 'Everyone calls him Bram outside the office, Ric,' she sidestepped lightly. 'What about tonight?' She injected eagerness into her voice. And wondered why she had to inject it.

'He's given you the night off as well? A *Saturday* night?' Richard sounded surprised.

'Well, sort of. I have to drive him to the opera house. But Ric, he's invited us both to join him for the evening. He has two spare tickets.'

'For the symphony concert?' Richard's voice brightened.

'No...to a play. An Ibsen play, I think he said.'

'Ibsen! Hell! Hardly our cup of tea.'

'We've never been to an Ibsen play, Ric. It'll be a new experience,' she said cajolingly, and heard what sounded like a snort.

'When I go out I prefer to be entertained, not wrung out. Can't we get out of it? Couldn't you drop him off there and pick him up later? We could go and see that new movie...the one with that hilarious little guy in it...what's his name?'

'We can go and see that any time.' Normally, Mia was happy to go along with Richard's wishes. She enjoyed a good comedy as much as he did. But this time, perversely, she dug her heels in. 'I'd *like* to go, Ric. We never go to the theatre—not to see a play, I mean. We never even see a serious, thought-provoking movie. It's always lightweight stuff. Adventures, comedies...'

'We go to symphony concerts...the opera... *They're* serious.'

'Yes, but we never try anything *different*. Like jazz. Musical comedy. Foreign films. A good play.'

'You've never complained before. I thought you enjoyed the things we do.'

'I did. I do. It's just that—there are other things...' She paused, sighing. 'Ric, it's jolly decent of him to invite us. He's offered us dinner as well.' And she added persuasively, 'It'll give you a chance to meet him.'

This was greeted with a grunt. But he gave in. 'OK, we'll go. You know I'd do anything for you. But don't let's make a habit of it...all right?'

'All right.' She felt absurdly pleased. She wasn't sure why. She sincerely hoped she wouldn't live to regret it. Dragging Richard along to an Ibsen play, which probably *would* be depressingly heavy. Suffering Bram Wild's grilling of Richard over dinner, knowing that he already thought Richard a bit of a wimp. How would the two get on? They were so different, such opposites!

Once he gets to know Richard, she thought loyally, Bram will see what a thoroughly nice person he is. Everybody likes Richard.

'I'll see you tonight, then,' she said warmly. 'I'll ring you later with the arrangements. Bye for now.'

When she popped out on to the terrace later to take her leave of Bram for the day he had already finished his breakfast and was leaning back in his cane chair, folding up his newspapers.

He glanced round. 'I take it you didn't want breakfast?' He glowered as he ran his eyes over her, and she felt her body stiffen. Why was he scowling at her? She wasn't interrupting his breakfast—he'd already finished. Surely he hadn't missed her company? He had had his papers to read!

'I did let Mrs Tibbits know,' she said defensively. 'I'm going to have breakfast with Diana, my flatmate, and her sister. And then I'm going to my mother's.' She had rung them both after speaking to Richard.

'You're not seeing your... fiancé?'

'Not until tonight. He's... busy.' She didn't go into details. It was none of his business! 'What time would you like me back this afternoon?' she asked.

'I want to leave here by six. The pre-theatre dinner starts at half-past.' His tone was curt. 'Will you and your fiancé be joining me for the evening?' His blue eyes were shadowed and remote. Indifferent.

Mia licked her lower lip. She was beginning to wonder why she had ever considered accepting his invitation. But she heard herself answering, 'Thank you...yes, we'd love to.' Hoping that by this evening he would be in a better humour.

'You'll take my car, of course.' He rose as he spoke, leaving the folded newspapers on the table.

'I was going to get a bus and pick up my own car from Di's.'

'Take mine.' It was an order. No arguments, his tone said.

'Very well. Have a good day,' she said sweetly, and turned away without waiting to see how her rather facetious farewell had affected his mood.

Moments later, as she was backing Bram's car out of the garage, a sleek gold Mazda pulled into the kerb and Bram's general manager, Russ Masters, waved at her through the window. By the time she had swung Bram's car out into the street, Russ was standing at her side window. His handsome face, above his striped T-shirt, was shaded by a floppy hat. He was, as usual, smiling.

'Good morning, Mia. Got the day off, have you?' As she nodded she realised he was staring at her. 'Goodness, Mia, you look so much like...' He stopped, his ready smile wavering.

She looked up at him. 'Like...?'

He looked as if he was trying to make up his mind whether to tell her or not. 'Like Natasha,' he said finally. And looked at her enquiringly, as if expecting her to be already familiar with the name. 'You look even more like her today, with your hair pulled back the way you have it now.'

Mia involuntarily raised a hand to her hair. After her shower this morning she had, in defiance of Bram Wild's wishes, decided against leaving it loose, and had pulled it back as before, only this time she had parted it in the middle, drawing it back in a demure Madonna-like style.

'Who's Natasha?' she asked cautiously.

'You mean you haven't heard about Natasha?' When she shook her head, Russ drew in his lips. 'Well...I guess there's no harm in telling you. You're bound to hear sooner or later, and best you hear it from me than from some...scandalmonger. Natasha was the girl Bram was going to marry. The great love of his life.'

Mia felt something flutter inside her. 'You mean...she died?'

'No.' Russ's voice hardened. 'She jilted him. Ran out on him three days before their wedding, and married someone else. An old childhood friend. They left Sydney and settled in Melbourne soon after they were married. It all caused quite a stir at the time.'

Mia felt tiny goosebumps break out on her skin. 'How...awful for him.'

'Yes. Terrible. I don't think he's ever really got over it. Not,' he added hastily, 'that he ever talks about it, not even to me. That's how I know it went deep. Of course, it all happened a long time ago. Years. He's had plenty of women since then. But they've all been...quite different from Natasha. And none of them have lasted long.'

'What was she like?' Mia asked. She found she was hardly breathing.

'She was like a breath of fresh air—very young, very warm, and very sweet. An exquisite little thing, slender as a reed. Lovely face, too. She looked a lot like you, Mia. Pale skin, delicate bones, clear eyes. Only her eyes were blue, from memory, not green.'

Mia, flushing faintly, was conscious of a faint sound, like the rapid beating of wings. She had always had the feeling there was something...

Russ gave a wry grin. 'Even her voice...it was soft and beautifully modulated...just like yours. And she always wore her hair pulled back the way you have yours today. It was a reddish colour too, come to think of it, though much paler than yours.'

Mia swallowed. 'So you knew her...personally?'

He nodded. 'I'd come to work for Bram shortly before they got engaged. I was going to be best man at their wedding.'

Mia asked slowly, her mind swinging back, 'Did Bev Loft know Natasha too?'

Russ looked surprised. 'I shouldn't think so. Bev wasn't around then. But she'd have heard about her...there's been enough talk over the years. Gossip, rumours...you know how it is. Everybody giving their own theories about what happened, and why.'

'Why...did it?' Mia asked tentatively.

He drew back a little. 'Only Bram and Natasha know the answer to that one. As I said, Bram never talks about it. Most people assume she ditched him because the other guy offered her more. He'd just inherited his father's millions—the Kennedy-Ford chemical empire.'

Mia digested that for a moment. 'And...what do other people assume was the reason?' she ventured. She knew she shouldn't be asking, but she wanted to know what was being said about her boss. Maybe it would help her to understand Bram a little better.

'There were those who said that Bram was after *her* money, and that she woke up to him in the nick of time.' Russ gave a snort to show what he thought of that idea. 'Her folk were well off too, you see...and well-known, socially. Old family name...that sort of thing. By marrying her, Bram would have had instant wealth *and* social standing. Bram didn't have either *then*...he was only just starting out in business. And his family were nobodies—simple country folk.'

'But you don't think——?'

'Of course I don't. It's all bunkum. Bram really loved that girl. I don't think he's ever got over her. You can't really blame him for swearing off marriage, or being cynical about women after what she did to him. Since Natasha, he's been careful never to let anyone get too close.'

'Do *you* think Natasha jilted him because this other man—Kennedy-Ford—offered her more?'

He gave a shrug. 'She never struck me as being the mercenary sort, but nothing else makes any sense. Ironical, isn't it? Bram is worth far more now than Kennedy-Ford ever was or ever will be. Bram would be quite a catch these days—if he wanted to be caught. Not that he shouts about what he's worth, or pushes himself into the limelight ... he prefers to let his achievements speak for themselves.'

'I wonder if she's ever regretted it,' Mia wondered aloud, looking beyond him, her eyes faintly pensive.

'Natasha?' Russ gave a shrug. 'By all accounts, she and her husband are perfectly happy. They've had a couple of kids. Maybe I'm doing her an injustice. She and Kennedy-Ford were childhood sweethearts before Bram came along ... maybe she decided she loved the guy after all.'

'And Bram just ... accepted it?' Mia found it hard to imagine a man like Bram Wild giving up the girl he loved without a fight.

Russ shrugged. 'Bram isn't a man who *meekly* accepts anything. But there was nothing he could do. She'd gone. She ran off and married this other guy, leaving only a note behind. Of course, there were some people who said ...'

Mia waited, but Russ was already visibly retreating from that line of thought. He coughed. 'Look, people will say anything when a thing like this happens. You wouldn't believe some of the rumours that flew around at that time. They were crazy. Ridiculous...'

When he didn't elaborate Mia asked curiously, 'Didn't he take any action? Try to put a stop to it?'

'Nobody printed the stuff. And you can't stop talk. Anyway, Bram left the country right after it happened. Went off to the States for a couple of years, leaving me in charge here. He only had one starch mill then. He came back a wealthy man. And he's kept on expanding and growing richer ever since.'

A driven man, Mia mused. That would explain the 'powerful urges' he had spoken about, that had driven him on. The urge, the need to show the girl he'd loved and lost what she had missed out on. And perhaps to show the world a thing or two as well.

Were those same powerful forces still driving him today? He was still expanding his empire. There was talk now about a new Italian venture. Had the need to do better and better become an obsession with him?

Or was he still in love with Natasha, still driven by the need to prove to her that he was better than anybody else, even though she was now happily married to the man she had jilted him for, and living in another state? Was he hoping, despite all that, that one day she might...?

She felt a faint stirring of sympathy for Bram, and quickly suppressed it, knowing he wouldn't want her pity, or anyone else's. He wasn't that kind of man.

'I'd better be off,' she said, feeling disloyal now for staying out here talking about Bram behind his back. He wouldn't take kindly to that either!

'And I'd better go in and see Bram.' Russ straightened. 'We have some business matters to thrash out, and then I'm taking him sailing. He wants to give his boat a run. My wife's away this weekend with the kids and it'll make a nice change from watching junior rugby!'

'It sounds fun.' Mia felt a sudden yearning to go with them, to go sailing for the first time in her life, to feel the wind through her hair, to enjoy yet another new experience. If she hadn't made plans to go and see Diana and her mother today would Bram have invited her to go with them?

She sighed. Probably not. He wouldn't want her around when he didn't need her. Not if she was so much like Natasha, the girl who had jilted him.

But if she did remind him of Natasha, and that most painful period in his life, why had he employed her in the first place? Could it mean that he was over her at last? Or...? Mia bit her lip as another more sinister possibility occurred to her. What if Bram, in some warped way, had come to see Natasha's face every time he looked into *her* face, so that each time he roared at her and bullied her he was in reality hitting back at Natasha, the woman who had run out on him? A man might get a kick, a kind of sadistic satisfaction out of imagining that he had the woman he despised at his mercy!

No, it was too sick! She dismissed the idea as ridiculous. Surely Bram Wild couldn't be that ruthless, that twisted? She was getting paranoid. In all likelihood, he saw no similarity between them whatsoever. Or if he did it no longer affected him, one way or the other. Surely he wouldn't have appointed her to the job if it did?

But, despite herself, she felt a tiny shiver of doubt.

*   *   *

She could feel Bram's narrowed eyes on her as she waved to Richard across the opera house foyer, where they had agreed to meet, and as she moved forward to greet her fiancé, raising her face for his kiss. For a reckless, yearning moment she wished that Richard would throw out his arms and wildly embrace her. But of course, he didn't . . . he merely bent his head and brushed her cheek with his lips. He had never liked displays of emotion in public. In private, either, for that matter. She had long ago learned to restrain her own natural exuberance when she was with him, just as she had learned to restrain it, for the most part, in her mother's presence.

'You're wearing your hair loose,' was the first thing he said. Accusingly, she thought.

'You sound like my mother,' she said lightly. 'She thinks I look like an abandoned woman when I wear my hair loose.'

'Then why wear it like that?'

'Oh, Ric! I got tired of pulling it back, that's all.' She had no intention of telling him the real reason. Especially with Bram Wild hovering behind.

She saw Richard's gaze flicker past her. 'Aren't you going to introduce me?'

'Yes . . . of course.' As she swung round to make the introductions she found herself watching them as they sized each other up, Richard, reserved and stiffly polite, immaculate in his dark suit and sober tie, Bram very much at ease in his suede jacket, casual trousers and tieless designer shirt, his face looking more tanned than ever after his day's sailing, his unruly hair curling over his collar in its usual disarray.

Mia was becoming used to it now. It suited him, she realised, somewhat to her own surprise. It was wild and untamed . . . like him. She tried to imagine Richard's hair

like that, and couldn't. Tonight, as usual, every hair on
his smooth fair head was neatly, slickly in its place. She
found herself idly wondering how it would look if she
ran her fingers through it. Richard would only smooth
it down again, she suspected ruefully. He hated looking
rumpled.

'Ready for dinner?' Bram asked, turning his head to
catch her eye. She blinked away her idle thoughts, and
nodded.

When they were shown to their table Mia managed to
manoeuvre herself so that she was sitting facing Richard,
not Bram. She knew she would feel more comfortable
that way. She always felt comfortable with Richard. He
was so solid and reliable and . . . safe. Bram Wild made
her feel anything *but* comfortable and safe.

At least Bram's mood, she was relieved to see, had
improved. She wondered if it was his day's sailing that
had done the trick, or if it could have anything to do
with the way she was wearing her hair this evening. She
had left it loose deliberately, not wanting it to remind
him of Natasha.

'Anyone care for the yabbies?' Bram asked as they
pored over the menu. His voice, Mia mused, was quite
spell-binding when he wasn't shouting or being sar-
castic. It was deep and vibrant and sensual, and that
faint lilt was intriguing.

'I will,' she said, surprising herself. 'I've never tried
yabbies.'

'One should try . . . everything,' Bram said, his eyes
faintly mocking. 'Richard?'

'I think I'll stick to the whiting.' Richard wasn't very
adventurous when it came to food. When it came to
anything, for that matter, Mia reflected with a faint sigh.

She found herself involuntarily comparing Richard's voice with Bram's. Richard had a pleasant voice—which wasn't surprising for someone who sang in a choir—but there wasn't anything particularly remarkable or riveting about it. But then, it was never harsh or insolent either—it was always mild and easy to listen to. And surely that's what counts in the long run? she thought loyally.

On the whole, it wasn't a bad evening. Bram went out of his way to make it easy for them. He seemed able to talk on any subject, and if one topic failed to ignite a spark in either of them he would swing smoothly to another. When, as happened once or twice, Richard probed delicately into Bram's business dealings, Bram responded easily and frankly, without blowing his own trumpet, but, Mia noticed, whenever Richard tried to broach the more personal aspects of the tycoon's life, Bram skilfully steered the conversation elsewhere.

She realised, after a while, that her earlier qualms about Bram had been unnecessary. Far from being his usual aggressive, insolent self and bombarding Richard with callous, humiliating questions, Bram seemed intent on not alarming or antagonising him, showing that he could, when he set his mind to it, be thoroughly charming. She saw Richard visibly relaxing under his spell. So much so that, by the end of the meal, Bram had, she perceived with some awe, managed to extract a good deal of information from Richard...about his work as a tax accountant, about his love for singing and classical music, about his collecting, and no doubt about his character as well!

Bram's being careful not to antagonise Richard because he doesn't want to risk losing his new driver, she concluded, and with it came a surge of resentment.

Bram still has doubts about me, she seethed inwardly. He still thinks I wouldn't be capable of standing up to Richard if Ric asked me to leave this job!

'Powerful stuff,' Bram commented when they emerged later from the drama theatre. 'What did you think of it?' he asked Mia.

'Brilliant. Everything about it.' The play had been quite an experience for Mia. But she could tell that Richard hadn't enjoyed it one bit, though he kept his thoughts to himself, remaining tight-lipped, with just an occasional mute nod while she and Bram were raving about the range and depth of the acting, the power of the story, and the stark brilliance of the sets.

'Let's have coffee back at my place.' Bram steered them towards the car park. 'You'll join us, Richard, won't you? It will give you a chance to see where Mia is living. Feel free to visit her whenever it's . . . convenient.'

Mia glanced at Richard, but couldn't quite catch his eye. She wondered if Richard knew that Bram meant when it was convenient to *him*, not to them.

'Thank you,' said Richard. 'If you give me your address I'll follow in my car.'

Mia bit on her lower lip. How stiff and starchy and formal he sounded! He'd been like it all evening. Or was he always that way and she'd never noticed before?

'You mean you haven't asked Mia where she is living?' Bram's blue eyes pierced Richard.

'I have a vague idea.' Richard looked uncomfortable now. 'I have her phone number,' he said defensively.

'Well, then, that's all that matters, isn't it?' said Bram, the sarcasm in his voice only marginally veiled.

'What a beautiful piano!' Richard's thin face lit up as he walked into Bram's spacious sitting-room and saw the gleaming baby grand, starkly black against the white drapes. 'Mia, have you played it yet?'

Mia flushed. 'Of course I haven't. I've never been in here before.' Had Richard forgotten she was just Bram's driver? Just his temporary personal assistant?

Richard looked a bit flustered. 'No, of course not . . . Er—do you play?' he asked Bram.

'Sadly, no. But I encourage my guests to. Feel free,' Bram invited. 'We could have a sing-along.'

Richard seemed not to sense the faint mockery in Bram's tone, just as he hadn't sensed his sarcasm earlier. 'Mia is the pianist, not me. But I'd be happy to sing for you.'

'Ric, Bram doesn't want——' Mia began.

'Oh, but I do. Please . . . I insist.' Bram was already sinking into one of his soft white leather settees. 'I'm sure you make a . . . perfect duo.'

Richard was already gravitating towards the piano, urging a reluctant Mia along with him. 'Let's do "La donna è mobile", from *Rigoletto*,' he suggested. 'It appeals to most people. And it's not too difficult to play . . . is it?' He was well aware that she wouldn't have practised for a while.

'No, it's not difficult,' agreed Mia, stifling a faint sigh. It wasn't absorbingly interesting to play, either. In fact, it was plain boring. Like a lot of Richard's accompaniments. But she sat down at the piano and dutifully played. Richard's singing was, as usual, faultless. His voice, which was more lyrical than robust, was tuneful and pleasant to listen to. In small doses, a capricious voice whispered.

When the song came to an end, Bram applauded warmly, pounding his good hand on the arm of the settee.

'Bravo!' he bellowed. 'You have a fine voice, Richard. But Mia, I hardly heard you. How about playing a solo?'

'Oh, no, I...'

'Please,' he insisted. Making it sound more a command than a request.

As she hesitated Richard said, 'Go on, Mia.' But he sounded a bit half-hearted about it. Mia knew he didn't see her as a solo pianist. She didn't come up to his meticulously high standard. Which was why she generally preferred to play when there was nobody listening. She could let her hair down then, and not worry about a few mistakes. 'Play that sweet little Debussy piece,' he coaxed.

Something inside Mia rebelled at that. How condescending Richard could be at times! Funny how she'd never noticed it before. It had been on the tip of her tongue to decline to play at all, but now, impelled by a rare imp of mutiny, she turned to the keyboard with new resolve and launched into a passionate Chopin polonaise. One she had always enjoyed playing in the privacy of her mother's living-room.

She really threw herself into it, playing with passion and gusto, blotting out the thought that Richard and Bram were listening. As a result, she surprised herself by playing it without a fault or a fumble.

As the final chord died away there was a moment of silence. Stealing a look round, she saw the flush of discomfort on Richard's face and knew that she had shocked him. He was always uncomfortable when she showed any undue display of passion... just as her mother was. Her mother was always afraid it was her wild father in her coming out.

She couldn't look at Bram. Had she shocked him too? Hardly, she thought scathingly. Bram Wild wasn't the type to be easily shocked. Certainly not by a piece of music!

'Brilliantly played, Mia!' Bram's rich voice broke the silence, and that was all he had a chance to say because Mrs Tibbits chose that moment to bring in their coffee. 'Richard, would you like a port?' Bram asked, hauling himself to his feet.

'No, thanks, Bram, I'm driving.'

'Why don't you drive home in the morning?' Bram suggested easily. 'I'm sure Mia would be delighted to accommodate you.'

Mia shot him a brief, virulent look as Richard said hastily, 'Thanks, but...' he gulped down his coffee '...it's time I was off... It's been a——'

'Oh, but surely you want to see Mia's apartment first?' Bram said languidly. 'If only to reassure yourself that she is...safe and private up there. Anyway, you must both be dying for some time together...alone.' His blue eyes glittered wickedly under the devilish eyebrows, and Mia almost choked on her coffee. The fiend! He knew perfectly well that they...that Richard...that the two of them had decided to wait until they were married before...

'I'm sure Mia's apartment is as fine as the rest of your house,' Richard assured him hastily, almost tripping over his feet as he rose from his chair. 'I'll see it some other time perhaps...when it's not so late.'

Mia stifled a sigh. He could at least have come up-stairs and had a *look*. He could at least have *pretended* that they were lovers! But of course, Richard would never do that. He was always so stiff and proper and...and moral. Not only was he determined that she should go to her wedding-day a virgin, but he was equally determined that she should be seen by the world to be a virgin!

Sometimes she wondered why she had gone along with his wishes for so long. But she knew in her deepest heart why she had. It wasn't only Richard and knowing that she would shock him to the core if she ever decided to throw herself at him in wild, passionate abandon. There was her mother, too. Her mother, who had never got over the shame of falling pregnant to Mia's father at the tender age of eighteen, or the knowledge that he had only married her because of pressure from her parents. To see her only daughter fall into the same pit would devastate her, even if this marriage was wanted by both parties.

'I'll see you out, Richard,' Mia said, a sigh in her voice.

'Why don't you both come sailing with me tomorrow?' Bram's voice halted them both in their tracks.

Richard blinked faintly. 'You . . . can sail a boat with your hand in plaster?'

One corner of Bram's mouth twisted slightly. 'I didn't do too badly today, with Russ's help. Tomorrow, if you're willing to lend me a pair of hands, I should be able to manage the boat without too much difficulty.'

'Oh, Ric, I'd love to go sailing!' Mia's delicate face glowed at the thought.

But Richard was shaking his head, looking regretful. A feigned regret, Mia suspected. 'I have to go to choir practice in the afternoon . . . and in the morning I was planning to go to an antique auction. I was hoping you'd come with me.' He looked appealingly at Mia.

Mia bit her lip. Bram, she noticed, was saying nothing at all. Was he waiting to see if she would stand up for

herself and do what she wanted to do? In the past she
would have gone happily along with Richard's wishes,
just so that they could be together. But...damn it, why
shouldn't she go sailing for once? Richard wouldn't miss
her—he'd have his head buried in musty antiques—and
in the afternoon he'd waltz off to his choir practice, and
she'd be left alone.

'Ric...' she took a deep breath '...Bram will need
me to—to help him on the boat.'

'Don't worry about me,' drawled Bram. 'There are
plenty of others who'd enjoy a day's sailing.'

'But I *want* to go.' Mia lifted her small chin.

Richard heaved a sigh. 'Well...why not?' he said with
a shrug. 'Maybe we could get together in the evening...'
He turned his head to look enquiringly at Bram.

'Sorry, we're off to Melbourne tomorrow night,' Bram
put in. 'I have an early-morning meeting on Monday.'
As Mia blinked at this piece of news, Bram went on,
'Look, Richard, why don't you come sailing with us in
the morning, and I'll drop you ashore in time for you
to get to your choir practice in the afternoon?'

Mia silently clapped her hands. What a wonderful
solution, she thought. She could have hugged Bram.

But Richard was shaking his head again. 'Thanks,
Bram, but I don't want to miss this auction... You go,
Mia, if you want to. I'll see you when...whenever,' he
finished lamely.

Mia didn't try to change his mind. She knew he'd hate
going sailing anyway. He'd be far happier among his
antiques.

'I'll come out to the car with you,' she said, tucking
her arm through his. 'Goodnight, Bram. It's been a
lovely evening.' And it had, for the most part.

'Come back and join me for a port, if you like,' Bram said wickedly, and she threw him a baleful look. What was he trying to do? Make Richard jealous?

'I'll see you in the morning,' she said firmly, and dragged Richard from the room.

CHAPTER FIVE

'OH, BRAM, this is wonderful!' Mia held her face into the wind, an uncontrollable smile on her lips. 'I never dreamed sailing could be such fun!'

It couldn't have been a better day for sailing. There was a good stiff breeze blowing, and just enough cloud cover to temper the hot March sun. The harbour was alive with colourful sails, chugging ferries, gleaming white motor cruisers—boats of all sizes and shapes.

'You mean you've honestly never sailed before?' The wind threw Bram's words back at her from his position at the wheel. He looked like a pirate today, Mia thought, with his white shirt slashed open to his waist, his bronzed chest gleaming, his bare legs braced wide apart, his head thrown back and his silver-streaked hair whipping wildly in the wind. Even his plaster cast failed to spoil the illusion—quite the reverse, in fact. He wore it like a badge of war, like a battle wound won in a cut-throat skirmish with rival pirates.

She shut her mind to the tawdry fist-fight that in reality must have caused the injury.

'Never!' she tossed back at him. She had crossed the harbour many times by ferry, and occasionally had skimmed across it in a water-taxi or in one of the speeding hydrofoils. But it had never felt anything like this. This was pure *exhilaration*.

She hadn't realised she had uttered the word aloud until Bram laughed—a rich, full-bodied sound, all the more remarkable for being so rare. We should go sailing more often, she thought, responding with a quick smile of her own, if it has this humanising effect on him.

'Beats aerobics class, doesn't it?' Bram shouted into the wind, and she had to agree with him. 'Pity your fiancé's not here to share your enjoyment.'

Still gripped by her present euphoria, she answered without thinking, 'I'm afraid Richard isn't a great one for physical activity,' only to promptly wish, when she saw Bram's lip curl, that she hadn't used those particular words. She knew what kind of physical activity it would have conjured up in Bram Wild's fertile mind!

'Ready to eat?' he asked, and she was grateful to him for changing the subject. 'You must be getting up an appetite.'

She hadn't even thought about it, although they had been out here on the harbour all morning. She had been enjoying herself too much, and even the times when Bram had torn at his hair and bellowed at her, hurling swear words she had never heard before, had failed to dampen her enthusiasm. On those occasions she had been quick to realise that she had turned the wheel the wrong way, or unfurled the wrong rope, or got in his way, or in some other way given him just cause.

'Ready when you are,' she shouted back, realising that yes, she *was* hungry. Starving, in fact!

Bram steered the boat into a quiet bay, flanked by steep sandstone cliffs, and with her help he lowered the sails and dropped the anchor. They were out of the wind here, in a secluded, tranquil haven, the only sounds the warbling of birds and the gentle lap-lap of water against the sides of the boat. Bram ordered her below to fetch the icebox Mrs Tibbits had packed for them.

'We'll eat up here on deck. A picnic lunch in the open air is more pleasant than being stuck down below. I suggest you put a hat on,' he added, noting the pink glow that was creeping into her cheeks. A singularly becoming glow, he found himself thinking.

'I will,' she agreed readily, relieved that she wouldn't have to be alone with him down in that confined space below. Not that I'm scared of being alone with him, she assured herself as she lowered herself down the steep stairs. It's just that he might revert to his old obnoxious, arrogant self down there, and I like the open-air Bram much better...

When she emerged with the icebox, a wide-brimmed hat shading her face, Bram remarked approvingly, 'For someone who looks so fragile and helpless, I must say you've been quite handy to have aboard.'

She set the icebox down, letting her hair spill forward over her face as she bent over, to hide a flush of embarrassment. Coming from Bram Wild, that was high praise indeed! 'I told you I'm stronger than I look,' was all she said, but she was secretly as pleased as punch. She had done all she could to pull her weight this morning, jumping to do whatever Bram commanded her to do, willing to try anything, doing the best she could in this strange new world of boats and sailing. It was good to know that, despite his occasional ranting, he considered she hadn't done too bad a job.

As she burrowed into the icebox, Bram's shadow fell over her and she felt a *frisson* of excitement quiver through her. She glanced up at him from beneath her sweep of lashes—unusually dark lashes for a redhead— and felt another tremor run through her when she met him eye to eye.

'Your eyes are shining like emeralds, Mia.' His smile was faintly mocking, but, other than that, his expression was inscrutable, his own eyes glittering enigmatically under the heavy winged brows.

She swallowed before trusting herself to speak. Because say something she must. She didn't want him thinking the glitter in her eyes had anything to do with him! Because it didn't...

'I can't remember the last time I had a picnic lunch,' she heard herself babbling, her gaze fluttering away from his.

'Richard doesn't care for picnics.' Bram made it a flat statement rather than a question.

She flushed. It was true, but she heard herself leaping to Richard's defence, clutching at her fiancé as she would clutch at a lifeline. 'Picnics don't appeal to everybody. A lot of people hate the wind and flies and the hot sun...'

'But they don't bother you?'

'Well, no... They're part of the fun.'

'You don't have much fun, do you, Mia?'

She couldn't look at him. 'We do... other things.'

'Things *you* want to do... or he wants to do?'

She shifted restlessly. 'Both,' she said, almost snapping the word. And then she heard herself gabbling, 'I go to my aerobics class without Richard, and I often take my mother for a weekend drive into the country without Richard, and I see my friends...' She let her voice trail off. Oh, lord, how unutterably boring all this must sound to a high-flier like Bram Wild!

'Riveting,' he commented drily, confirming what she'd just thought. 'I'd say you've been missing out on a lot, Mia.' His arm brushed hers, causing a prickle of sensation along her bare skin as he reached for something in the icebox, obviously not interested in her reply. Anyway, what answer could she give? She was beginning to agree with him! 'You must try Mrs Tibbits's excellent terrine, Mia,' he said, extracting it from the box. And a moment later, 'You can do the honours with the wine.'

She nodded, and obliged. With the ice-cold Sauvignon Blanc poured into chilled glasses, they tucked into the delicious feast of cold meats, crisp raw vegetables, and devilled eggs that Mrs Tibbits had prepared for them, making desultory conversation as they ate. Mia was just beginning to relax and enjoy herself again when he spoilt it.

'Why are you marrying him, Mia?'

She drew in a sharp breath, nearly choking on a mouthful of bread roll. She could feel his eyes boring into her face, and the glib 'Because I love him' died on her lips. Bram Wild, she sensed, wouldn't be satisfied with platitudes, no matter how true. She would have to come up with something a little more specific.

'Is it some kind of martyr thing?' he pressed.

'Certainly not,' she flashed back, tossing the remainder of her bread roll to the wheeling seagulls. 'Richard is a wonderful man and he'll make a wonderful husband.' Be *specific*, Mia, she urged herself impatiently. She cast around for the right words to describe him. 'He's a good man... there's not an ounce of malice in him. He's solid and dependable and trustworthy and——'

'Is that what you want?' Bram cut in, his mouth twisting. 'Not love, or passion, or excitement——'

'I do love him,' she cried, turning away from him and starting to repack the icebox. Anything to avoid his eyes!

'But not with passion or excitement...'

She scrambled to her feet, jutting out her chin, not sure how to reply honestly to that one. Her mother had always said that passion and excitement were not to be trusted...they didn't last...they only led to trouble and heartbreak. But sometimes she wished...

'What makes you think that?' she hedged, brushing the crumbs from the front of her blouse.

'I've seen you with him, remember? He could have been your brother, and you his sister, for all the emotion the two of you showed last night.'

'Our feelings are not for public scrutiny,' she flung back at him, her cheeks afire now.

'No?' He rose to his feet also, dwarfing her as they stood facing each other. 'You weren't afraid to show your feelings at the piano last night. You showed more passion playing that Chopin polonaise than you showed when you met your fiancé after an absence of a couple of days.'

'That's...different,' she protested. 'Richard and I...we don't like displaying our feelings in public. It doesn't mean we don't *have* strong feelings for each other.'

'Doesn't it?' His eyes were piercing hers, stripping her psyche bare. 'I don't think he'd be any different, even in the privacy of your own bedroom—if he's ever entered it, which I doubt. A man like that... he won't change, Mia, even when he marries you. He'll still be the self-centred, colourless wimp he is now. There's no fire in him, no passion. But I think there is... in you. Let's find out, shall we?'

She had no time to react. Before she could move away he had imprisoned her, one arm, the one in the plaster cast, sliding round her shoulders, moulding her to him, his other hand lacing through the tumbled mass of her hair, dislodging her hat and sending it sailing in a graceful, fluid movement to the deck. His fingers fastened on her head and drew her face towards his own, his lips towards her mouth, as inexorably as thunder follows lightning.

It all happened so quickly that she was powerless to resist, her body bending backwards beneath the assault. It was an explosive, seductive kiss, his tongue thrusting deep into the warm depths of her mouth, forcing her soft lips to part, his mouth smothering hers with such demanding mastery that she could scarcely breathe.

She gasped as he drew back just far enough to growl against her bruised lips, 'Has he ever kissed you like this, Mia?' and then he was kissing her again, plundering her lips like the pirate he had earlier reminded her of, his plaster cast hard on her back while the hand entangled in her hair freed itself and began to fumble with the buttons of her blouse.

From somewhere, way down in the deepest recesses of her being, she felt a shudder of response, a feeling she had never experienced with Richard, and she thought, No! and began to fight, her heart churning, her blood at fever-pitch. But she had no strength, her legs seemed to have turned to water, and an exquisite helplessness was sweeping over her, a new sensation that pierced her deep inside, and left her powerless to fight him.

'Or touched you . . . like this?' His hand slipped inside her blouse and brushed over the silky mound of her breast, above the frothy lace of her bra, his fingers gently tugging at the flimsy fabric, feeling for the rosy peak below. When he found what he was looking for, and his fingertips began to circle and tease, she felt an exquisite tingling sensation as the tip of her breast sprang to life under his touch, arousing her from the lethargy she had fallen into. Instinctively her back arched and her body strained against his, the painful tightening of newly aroused flesh sending shock-tremors through her.

As if her voice belonged to someone else, she let a soft moan escape her lips, and that seemed to act as a kind of signal. Hearing it, Bram jerked back, withdrawing his hand as if it were on fire, thrusting her away from him.

'There!' There was a ragged triumph in the harsh utterance, a veiled darkness in his eyes as he stepped back with a muttered, 'I rest my case...' his lip curling cruelly as he turned sharply away from her, showing her in no uncertain terms that his kiss had been merely a demonstration, that he hadn't meant it to be taken personally.

'How—how dare you?' she gasped belatedly, her legs caving in under her now that he was no longer holding her upright. She sank down on to the bench seat and sagged against the hard wooden bow of the boat, chest heaving, cheeks flushed, valiantly trying to mask her inner turmoil behind a show of fuming indignation. Indignation and anger being easier to deal with than other emotions he had aroused.

She might as well not have spoken. 'Get that icebox down below and then come back and hold the wheel for me,' he rapped over his shoulder as he started hauling at the anchor, with little regard for his broken hand. 'We've just got time to sail back to my place, pack, and get to the airport.'

Though their only conversation on the way back was to shout orders and responses at each other, the sail back across the harbour acted as a balm to her shattered nerves, and by the time they stepped ashore she was able to face him without wavering when he asked abruptly, 'Do you have any friends or relatives in Melbourne?'

'I have an aunt...'

'They why don't you ring her before we go and see if you can spend the evening with her? I'll be having dinner with an old friend... I won't need you until the meeting tomorrow morning.'

A woman friend, no doubt... Mia put the tightening in her throat down to scorn. As if he needs to throw his women in my face! I'm well aware that that kiss of his didn't mean anything. It was just meant to show up Richard. Just meant to humiliate me, because the man can't bear the thought of anyone being happy, after what Natasha did to him.

As she thought of Natasha a niggling suspicion surfaced. Natasha lived in Melbourne. Was *she* the old friend Bram was planning to meet for dinner? Had he successfully managed to woo her back into his life? Secretly, behind her husband's back? Was he hoping—contriving—to destroy Natasha's marriage? Mia's slim hand fluttered to her throat. If that was his aim what powerful urges were motivating him this time? Love? Or... revenge? Did Bram still want Natasha... or was he planning to win her back and then dump her, the way she had once dumped him...?

He would be ruthless enough, Mia decided. He can't bear to see anyone settled and happy! That's why he's trying to thrust a wedge between Richard and me...

Well, he won't succeed, she vowed, clenching her small fists until her knuckles turned white. I love Richard and I'm going to marry him! I *am*!

She realised she was trembling all over, and began to twist Richard's diamond ring round and round her finger, as if by touching his ring she could come closer to him, and find some peace.

Bram Wild is *evil*, she thought fiercely as she escaped to her room to pack an overnight bag. His whole outlook on life and love has been twisted by what Natasha did to him. The man is capable of anything!

On the flight to Melbourne Bram extracted some papers from his briefcase and virtually ignored her for the full hour's flight, waving aside any offers of refreshments with a muttered, 'You don't want anything, do you? We'll both be having dinner when we get there.'

Mia shook her head, and kept her gaze fixed to the window, relieved that it was a clear day so that she had something to look at down below. It was only when the Airbus was coming in to land that she tensed in her seat, gripping the arm rest on either side as the plane banked sharply.

'You're not used to flying?' Bram turned to face her, as if he had sensed her tension.

'I haven't flown... much,' she admitted. 'It's only landing that bothers me. While I'm up in the air I'm fine.'

As she spoke he brought his left hand up to cover hers, closing over it so that she could feel the heat flowing from his hand into hers, a spasm shooting through her at his touch, riveting her body with threads of sensation. She found she couldn't move, couldn't speak.

'It's all right,' he said, mistaking her reaction for fear of the landing. 'Plenty of people feel the way you do. Have you ever travelled overseas, Mia?' She knew that he was only talking to reassure her, to keep her mind off their descent. But all she was conscious of now was the sensation of his hand on hers.

'A... a couple of times,' she said, unsticking her tongue, striving to keep her voice steady.

'You've been to Europe? The States?' She heard the surprise in his voice, and felt a warmth seeping into her cheeks.

'New Zealand,' she said. 'And Fiji.'

'That's all?'

She nodded, her mouth tightening.

'Oh, Mia.' She wasn't looking at him, but she knew he was shaking his head. 'There is so much you haven't done, haven't seen!'

She tilted her small pointed chin. 'There's plenty of time.' But *was* there? a restless voice inside her niggled. What time would she have if she married Richard and started a family straight away? It would be years before she and Richard could make an overseas trip...even if she could persuade him to go. Thus far, travel outside Australia had never appealed to him.

'You went with Richard?' Bram was asking.

She tugged at her lip with her teeth. 'I went to Fiji with Diana. And to New Zealand with my mother and brother Paul.'

'Not with Richard.' A derisive statement of fact.

'No.'

There was a gentle thud as the plane's wheels touched the tarmac. As the Airbus rolled towards the terminal she realised that Bram's hand was still covering hers. With flaming cheeks, she tugged it free.

'I'll get the bags down,' she said as the plane came to a halt. She could still feel a burning sensation where his hand had rested on hers. Incredible, but true.

She didn't have to make conversation on their way into town, because Bram chatted with their taxi-driver all the way from the airport to the Hyatt. Bram had booked them into opposite rooms on the same floor, but she had no reason to be apprehensive because they both went their separate ways minutes after their arrival, she catching a taxi to her aunt's place for dinner, and Bram to... wherever. She didn't see him again until breakfast the next morning, and he made no mention of where he had been the night before, or who with, and she certainly wasn't going to ask. She tried to read something in his face, in his manner, but detected no marked change in him.

They were both back in Bram's Sydney office by early afternoon, their Melbourne meeting having wound up by late morning and Bram not having bothered to stay for lunch, which they had on the plane. Mia found it hard to believe she was now sitting in Bram's office taking dictation, as if she had never been away. The life of the high-powered business executive was quite giddying! Not that she felt in any way fatigued. Far from it. She felt more wide awake, more alert, more *alive* than she had felt for years.

Richard noticed it that night, when she dropped in to see him at his flat, having rung first on Bram's car phone to make sure he'd be there. She had already dropped Bram off at a private function he had to go to, and she wouldn't be needed again until eleven.

'I've an hour to spare before I go to choir practice,' Richard said when she rang. 'We're having them every night now until we leave for our tour on Thursday. Why don't you pick up a pizza on your way over? I'll toss a salad.'

Over their pizza and salad Richard said, 'You look... different, Mia.' He frowned into her face. 'It's not your hair this time... it's *you*. There's a... sort of glow about you.'

'I got a bit burnt out on the harbour yesterday...'

'No, it's more than that.' He compressed his lips. 'That man...Bram Wild...he hasn't...*tried* anything, has he?'

'Tried anything?' Oh, lord, did it *show*?

'I've heard some pretty wild stories about him, Mia. He's a womaniser...women are just playthings to him. He uses them and then tosses them aside...the way some woman once tossed him aside. Virtually at the altar.'

'My. You have been doing your homework.'

'You're my future wife, Mia. Naturally I was anxious to know the kind of man you were working for. And now, having met him...'

'Yes?'

'I don't trust him, Mia,' he said, frowning. 'There's a restlessness, a wildness about him. And when he turns on the charm—well, he even charmed *me*. He's also rich and powerful—and a bachelor. A woman could find all that...irresistible.'

'I'm just working for him, Richard, nothing else.' *Nothing?* She remembered Bram's passionate kisses yesterday, and a rush of light-headedness swept over her. No, she thought, grasping at normality, at the cold hard facts. What happened yesterday didn't count, it didn't mean a thing. It had been meant as a demonstration—it hadn't been a come-on. Best to forget it had ever happened, to blot it from her memory—forever.

'I love *you*, Richard,' she asserted. 'We're engaged to be married. And Bram knows that. So you've no need to worry.' She wished her voice held more conviction. Why *didn't* it?

'Too bad I have to go away for a few days,' Richard said gloomily. He reached across the table for her hand. It was the first time he had shown any compunction, any regret about leaving her. Was it because, for the first time, he felt unsure of her?

'Ric, you've been looking forward to this Easter trip with your choir for weeks...' He couldn't actually be *jealous*, could he? He'd never shown a spark of it before. Would he fight for her, she mused, if he thought he had competition?

'That was before...' He withdrew his hand, and sighed. 'I feel as if you're slipping away from me, Mia. You don't seem to be the same girl any more...'

'Oh, Richard, of course I'm the same girl. Just because I've been doing a few new, different things lately it doesn't mean *I'm* different.' No? Would she be prepared to swear to that?

'I always knew where I was with you before,' he said plaintively. 'Now I don't. I'm not sure we like the same things any more... *want* the same things. You used to be happy just to be with me...'

She felt a swift stab of disappointment. He wasn't thinking of *her*, or what *she* might want—he was only thinking of himself, and how her new lifestyle was affecting *him*. Stung, she heard herself blurting out, 'Perhaps I've discovered that there's more to life than following you around like a puppy-dog all the time!' The second the words were out she sucked in her breath, aghast. What had got into her? She and Richard never fought!

Richard looked pained. 'It's him, isn't it?' he said bitterly. 'He's turned your head. With his sumptuous home and his jet-setting lifestyle and his millions. You're not content with the simple things of life any more... now that you've had a taste of the high life!'

'Oh, Ric, that's not true! Money and possessions don't come into it!' What could be more simple, she wanted to shout at him, than dawn rides in the park, and watching the sun rise, and picnic lunches, and sailing on the harbour? 'Ric, don't let's fight. You'll be going away in a few days...'

He stared at her across the table, his face taut. 'What will *you* be doing over Easter?' It was the first time he had bothered to ask.

She took a deep breath. 'Bram said something about me driving him up to the Blue Mountains. His sister lives up there.' As she said it her memory stirred. Hadn't Bram said that his sister was away overseas? Could she have come back already? Or was the house going to be un-occupied over Easter? *Just what did Bram Wild have in mind?*

She felt a shiver of panic, and reacted without thinking, scraping back her chair and diving at Richard, tugging him to his feet.

'Ric, I'm going to miss you!' she gasped, a faint thread of hysteria in her voice. It will be all right, she told herself fiercely. I love Richard, and he loves me, and we're going to get married just as soon as this job of mine is fin-ished. No matter what Bram Wild does or says, nothing is going to change that!

Richard looked startled as she wound her arms round his neck, bringing his own arms cautiously round her slim body as if he wasn't altogether sure what she had in mind. She stood on tiptoe, her eyes shimmering with confused emotions, her face upturned to his.

'Kiss me, Ric!'

'But it's——'

'Kiss me!'

Her fingers were applying pressure to the back of his head, pulling his face closer. Feverishly, she pressed her lips to his, urging a response, until finally his mouth began to move over hers, his arms tightening around her. She forced her lips apart, at the same time straining her body against his, the way she remembered straining against Bram Wild, trying to feel what she had felt in Bram's arms.

She felt nothing! She was conscious only of the movement of Richard's mouth, moist and warm and rather clumsy on hers, failing to arouse the faintest response in her. She clutched him tighter, desperate now, and she heard a grunt of protest as he dragged his mouth away from hers.

'Mia, what's got into you——?'

The doorbell shrilled and he jerked his head round, a flush spreading over his face as he extracted himself from her grasp.

'That'll be Jenny.' He ran the back of his hand over his lips, and reached up to smooth his hair. 'She said she'd come and pick me up. Seemed silly to take two cars when I'm on her way.' Was that faint relief she saw in his eyes as he swung away from her? And what other emotions did he feel, that he was trying to hide? Embarrassment? Distaste? Shock? Whatever it was, it didn't appear to be rapture, or passion... not even disappointment at being interrupted.

A strange resignation descended over Mia as she followed him to the door.

When she picked up Bram at eleven, after spending an hour or so with her mother, who was anxious to hear all about her evening with Aunt Margaret in Melbourne, Bram was in an unusually lazy, expansive mood and didn't seem to notice that she was rather quieter than usual. Obviously, he'd had a better evening than she'd had! A woman, no doubt, Mia concluded sourly. Yet another notch on the Wild scoreboard.

For the first time, she was aware of the smell of alcohol on his breath, and felt a quiver of unease. But her qualms soon subsided. While alcohol could, she knew, affect some men badly, turning even mild men into monsters, with Bram it seemed to have the opposite effect, loosening him up instead, and making him, if anything, *gentler*, more amiable. And he certainly wasn't drunk, or slurring his words, which were as crisp and clear as always.

So that when he invited her to have a nightcap with him on the front terrace, she found herself agreeing, deciding that it might help her to unwind, and to sleep more soundly afterwards.

He poured the drinks himself, not wanting to disturb Mrs Tibbits, who had already retired for the night. A Scotch on the rocks for him, a more diluted whisky for her.

'Just smell those roses!' he commented as they sank into the cushioned cane chairs on the moonlit terrace, overlooking the dancing lights of the harbour. The scent was wafting up from the garden below, the sweet fragrance as intoxicating as the whiskies they were drinking. As Mia's mind threw up the comparison she felt a renewed tingle of apprehension. If Bram was already mildly intoxicated, how would a few more whiskies affect him?

'Ever tried to count the stars?' Bram was asking.

'N-never,' she admitted, and gave a slightly fractured laugh. She wasn't really in the mood for laughter or jesting just now. Or for dealing with inebriated bosses, come to that. She had other more important things on her mind. Like her entire future! She stared up at the dazzling night sky, at the myriad twinkling stars, and stifled a sigh.

'By Sunday that moon will be a full moon.' Bram's voice rumbled into the silence.

'Oh, yes...Easter.' Mia knew her voice sounded flat, but she couldn't help it. She felt flat. Flat and unsettled, her mind in turmoil. What was she going to do about Richard? Why had she felt nothing tonight when he'd kissed her? Why had she only ever felt sweet, chaste emotions for him, and never a spark of what she had felt in Bram's arms? Why had she failed to arouse any real passion in Richard? Was all he wanted from her companionship, loyalty, lukewarm affection? She wanted more than that. Far more!

'You're very quiet, Mia.'

She started, and glanced round, to find Bram staring at her. Tension gripped her, and she was relieved that he hadn't switched on any of the outside lights. The moon, though bright, cast a softer, less revealing glow.

'I'm just a bit tired,' she said, striving to keep her voice steady. 'It's been a long day.'

'And a torrid evening?' he taunted softly. 'I guess you and lover-boy were anxious to make up for lost time...mm? I hope you weren't disappointed!'

His gibes touched her on the raw. Her pent-up tension snapped. 'Damn you, Bram Wild!' she burst out, springing to her feet. 'You won't be satisfied until you've driven us apart, will you? Well, let me tell you... if you think that kiss of yours is going to turn me against Richard you have another think coming! I loathe and detest you, Bram Wild, and all men like you!'

She was lashing out blindly, hardly knowing what she was saying, wanting only to wipe that smirk off his face, to show him that he was nothing to her, and never would be. 'You're nothing but a—a rake and a philanderer, and you have no real feelings left inside you any more!

If you think I want Richard to be like you you must be m-mad!'

Choking back a sob, she threw her glass down, beyond caring when it crashed into glassy fragments on the ceramic tiles. She whirled past him, streaking through the open front door and slamming it shut behind her.

CHAPTER SIX

BY THE time Mia reached her room the tears were flowing unchecked. She was already regretting her outburst, and her tears were as much for her job, which must now be in dire jeopardy, as for her frenzied, unpardonable outburst.

Bram would never forgive her! How had she dared to say what she had? And especially to a man who'd been drinking all evening. How would that affect his reaction? Slim chance that it would dull his responses and make him more reasonable. More likely it would sharpen them, causing a violent backlash!

Groaning, she threw herself down on the bed, her shoulders shaking with deep, convulsive sobs.

She didn't know how long she lay there, but eventually she dragged herself to her feet and stumbled into the bathroom to splash her face with cold water. Then she undressed and slipped on a filmy silk nightgown she had bought only the other day in a fit of madness. It felt wonderfully light and cool as it rippled sensuously over her heated skin, its luxurious silkiness helping to soothe her fractured nerves.

But the calming effect lasted only for a moment. She jumped as a sharp tapping sound shattered the evening silence. It seemed to be coming from...

Heat rushed to her face, and she leapt into the adjoining living-room, darting a look at the door which led out on to the balcony. As she had suspected, the tapping sound was coming from there!

'Wh-who is it?' she gasped, barely breathing.

'It's me...Bram.' He wasn't shouting—it was more a loud whisper. An *urgent*, demanding whisper. Of course, he wouldn't want to wake Mrs Tibbits!

A spasm of fear shot through her. What was Bram doing out there? What was he planning to do? Bawl her out? Wring her neck? Throw her out?

'Wh-what do you want?' she asked warily.

'Let me in, damn it! You locked me out!'

Her hand flew to her mouth. Of course! She had slammed the front door behind her. But...

'Surely you have a key? Where's Alf?' she croaked, the riotous beating of her heart almost deafening her.

'I gave Alf the night off. And if I had a key on me I'd use it. For goodness' sake, Mia, let me in! I don't want to disturb Tibby.'

What choice did she have? 'All right!' Swallowing, she darted forward, unlocked the door, and leapt back as he pushed it open and strode in.

He halted inside the doorway, his smouldering gaze sweeping over her, making her shrinkingly aware that she was wearing nothing but a flimsy wisp of silk. His brows were drawn, shadowing his eyes, and there was a tightness round his mouth, a muscle flicking at his jaw, as if he was trying to control some simmering—murderous?—emotion inside him. Perhaps he was silently counting to ten to keep himself from seizing her and shaking her. Or *worse*. She raised a bare arm as if to fend him off.

His voice split the silence. 'For pity's sake, Mia, stop cowering. What are you afraid of, for heaven's sake— that I'm going to clobber you?'

'You clobbered someone once before,' she shot back, a wary eye on his plaster cast.

He swore softly under his breath, and muttered drily, grinding the words through his teeth, 'If you go on standing in front of that lamp, Mia, with that wispy thing you're wearing doing absolutely nothing to hide every delectable contour of your body, I'll be wanting to do more than clobber you.'

She gasped and made a dive for her bedroom, her eyes searching frantically for a robe. When Bram followed her into the room she spun round to face him, her face flaming, her eyes wide and dark against the whiteness of her face.

'Don't you dare touch me!'

'What are you afraid of, Mia?' His eyes were mocking her now. 'That you might feel what you felt before?' He was moving closer as he spoke, advancing slowly, inexorably towards her. '*He's* never made you feel like that...has he? He's never made you feel anything...except warm and comfortable, perhaps. You can't tell me that's what you want.'

'How would you know what I want?' She spoke scathingly, wanting to throw up a wall between them, at the same time snatching up her robe from the back of a chair, and bundling it round her.

'You can't fool me, Mia. You're not the demure little thing you try to make out. I've seen evidence of it, remember? You'll never be happy with a milksop like Richard. There's too much fire and passion in you. It's all bottled up inside you, simmering to come out, to send you to heights you never dreamed of...'

'Or depths,' she shrilled, thinking of her mother. Her mother had given in to mindless passion once—just once in her life—and it had led to nothing but heartbreak and bitterness.

He paused, a few paces away from her. 'You think you'll be content with a life that's going to bore you to death, Mia, that's always going to be smooth and cosy and comfortable? Some women might be content with a life like that, but not you, I think. You strike me as a woman who wants more from life. Think of your life with Richard so far. Where are the peaks and troughs that make a relationship real and exciting? Where are the dizzy heights of passion?'

'I don't want peaks and troughs; I don't want passion,' she cried desperately, clasping her chest as if by doing that she could stop her heart's erratic pounding. 'I—I want something deeper and more lasting. Like what my mother had with my...my father.' She gulped, and went on breathlessly, 'Theirs was a gentle, enduring love, which lasted until he died. I'll have the same kind of life with Richard. Steady and solid and—and satisfying.'

'*Satisfying?* Who are you trying to convince, Mia? Me—or yourself? You're not your mother. I'd say your needs are quite different, from what I know of you. Don't try to be something you're not.'

Mia turned away from him, chewing on her lip. Every word he uttered was striking a chord inside her, but she couldn't admit it...she wouldn't! It went against everything her mother had drummed into her over the years. Passion was dangerous, not to be trusted, it didn't last... Reliability and stability and mutual respect were what counted. Mia had always tried to accept that, to believe it was true.

At a sound behind her, she whirled back to face him, only to see him reaching out to pick up a framed photograph from the chintz-covered dressing-table.

'Is this your mother?'

She nodded.

'You don't look at all like her. You must look like your father.'

A faint shadow flitted across Mia's face. Was she like her father? How would she know? She couldn't remember him—her real father—well enough to say, except that he must have had red hair too, because her mother had said to her once, when Mia had lost her temper over something, 'You don't get your temper from me...you must get it from him. It's the red hair. Let's hope that's all you've inherited from him.' And from then on her mother had insisted on Mia plaiting her hair or tying it back, as if by confining it she could somehow diminish its power, its unacceptable effect on her daughter.

Bram's hand came up to brush her cheek in a gesture of comfort, and she jumped at his touch, as if his fingers had burnt her skin. He was looking at her oddly, and no wonder. He must be wondering why on earth she had plunged into a black reverie over a perfectly natural observation. For a brief moment she was tempted to tell him about her father—her real father—but the thought of Bram's probable reaction held her back. She knew what he'd say. Gloatingly. 'Ah, so that's where you get it from...your passion, your restlessness, your zest for life.' She had no wish to be anything like the father she had been brought up to despise, the father who had walked out on his wife and child after a bare two years of marriage, only to leave the country and never be seen again, never to acknowledge his daughter from that day on.

Bram's hand slid to her shoulder, and his thumb-tip began to idly trace a pattern on the pale skin of her neck. She was vividly, suffocatingly aware of every tiny movement.

'You must have been very close to your father,' he said, misinterpreting her silence, her obvious pain. He was thinking of her *stepfather*, of course, who had died. He thought she was still grieving for *him*. Well, perhaps it was easier to let him go on thinking that. It wasn't as if he needed to know about her real father. Bram would be out of her life in a few weeks.

Why did the thought cause a twinge of pain?

She knew she ought to be shaking his hand away, but a strange paralysis seemed to have rendered her incapable of moving. After what seemed an eternity it moved away of its own accord, brushing her robe aside so that it slithered to the floor in a silky heap. His fingertips trailed down her bare arm, and it seemed that every tiny hair in their path was springing to vivid life at the contact. She felt her palms break out in a sweat and her knees begin to tremble. She couldn't let it go on! It mightn't be doing anything to him, but it was driving her crazy!

'Bram, I—I never should have said what I did...before.' The words burst out of her. Anything to break the spell!

'No?' His fingers closed on her arm, and they were none too gentle now, holding her in a grip of steel. There was a harshness in his voice as he barked at her, 'You said something about me having no real feelings *any more*. What did you mean by "any more", Mia? You think I had feelings once, do you?'

His compelling blue eyes shafted hers, daring her to hold back what she knew. She flicked a nervous tongue over her lips.

'I—I know about Natasha,' she whispered, knowing it would be futile to lie to him. 'Bram, I'm sorry...'

Apprehensive as she was, her warm heart went out to him.

She caught her breath as his hand tightened on her arm, hurting her now. His face had darkened, and he looked for a second as if he were about to take a swipe at her with his plaster cast. But he gave her a tiny shake instead with the hand that was still gripping her arm, and thrust his face closer, so that she could smell the whisky on his breath. Her lips parted, a new fear catching in her throat. How many whiskies had he had before he'd made his way up here?

'I don't need your sympathy, or anyone else's,' he grated, his eyes like shards of ice. 'And, if you want to know if I have any feelings left, try this!' His mouth came down on hers, brutally, stopping her breath, and, with his hand still clasping her arm and his muscular body pressing against hers, he pushed her mercilessly back until her legs were pinned against the side of the bed. There was nowhere further to go, and under his relentless pressure she lost her balance and fell back on to the bed, with Bram on top of her.

Under his crushing weight, she could feel the heat of his body burning through the flimsy silk of her skimpy nightgown. His plaster cast had missed her face by a whisker, and lay across the bed, close to her cheek, his other arm pinning her shoulder to the bed. His mouth was still firmly in possession of hers, his lips hard, relentless, hungrily demanding a response, and, despite herself, she felt a betraying flame lick through her body, even as she squirmed and struggled beneath him. His only response was to roll his body partially off hers, perhaps not wanting to crush her to death, but he kept one muscled leg sprawled across her and his hand immovable on her shoulder, effectively holding her captive. All the while keeping his bruising lips locked to hers.

For what seemed an eternity the deep, drugging kisses went on, his mouth smothering hers, his tongue feverishly tracing the soft fullness of her lips. She could feel her own treacherous response, and there was nothing she could do about it. Dimly, she was aware of his hand releasing its pressure on her shoulder and brushing down her body with exquisite slowness to explore the soft lines of her waist, her hips, through the wisp of silk covering them. Her senses reeled, threatening to spin her into dangerous oblivion, and it was only the smell of the whisky on his breath, foggily penetrating her consciousness, that gave her the strength to pull back from the precipice and start fighting anew, struggling for breath as she tried to wrench her mouth from his.

Finally he raised his head just far enough to growl tauntingly, 'What are you afraid of, Mia? Me...or yourself?'

Gasping to reinflate her lungs, she croaked, 'Neither! You—you've been drinking! You don't know what you're doing!'

He froze, his face swimming above her, his eyes dark shimmering pools with a glint of—what? Surprise? Anger?—in their depths. She bit her lip, bracing herself for his reaction.

After a long breathless moment he rolled away from her and hauled himself off the bed, his shoes making a soft thud as they touched the floor. More tense seconds ticked by as he stood looking down at her, his eyes glowing with a savage inner fire, his hair wild and tumbled above the dark devil's eyebrows. As she looked warily up at him he gave a harsh, contemptuous laugh.

'No need to worry, Mia, I wasn't about to lose control. I don't ravish virgins! Even after a few whiskies. You were quite safe, I assure you!' And with that he turned on his heel and left her, vanishing through the door without a backward glance.

Mia slept in the next morning, exhausted physically and emotionally, only waking when Mrs Tibbits drew back the heavy drapes, letting a flood of sunlight stream into the room.

She sat up abruptly, blinking at her bedside clock. She blinked again, in disbelief. It was after eight o'clock!

'I've missed breakfast!' she cried in dismay. 'I'm so——'

Mrs Tibbits cut her apology short. 'Mr Wild didn't want to disturb you earlier. He said you needed the extra rest.' Her face was impassive as she turned and picked up a tray from the dressing-table. 'He asked me to bring your breakfast up to you.'

'Oh . . . thank you.' Mia's brow puckered. Was Bram really being considerate? Or was he simply trying to avoid meeting her over breakfast, after what had happened last night? Or perhaps he had a massive hangover and was still in bed himself!

'Where is . . . Mr Wild?' she asked cautiously.

'He's out taking a walk. He's already had his breakfast, and read his papers. He's always an early riser.'

Mia shook her head, bemused. Did nothing affect that man? Not alcohol, not remorse, not anything?

It didn't seem to, because when she joined him shortly before nine o'clock to drive him to the office he acted as if nothing had happened between them, and all the way to the office, while she was negotiating the heavy peak-hour traffic, he chatted inconsequentially about the weather and items of current news, so that, by the time they strolled into the office together, her nerves had relaxed sufficiently to greet Bev Loft without any betraying tension.

It was a busy day. Bram had an important meeting the following day with the Premier on an environmental matter, and much of the day was spent preparing Bram's side of the case. They didn't even take a lunch break, Bram having sandwiches and fresh fruit brought into the office. She had no time to think about anything other than work.

But during the afternoon something happened to shatter the tenuous calm that had settled over her.

Bev put a call through to Bram's office, and Bram waved to her to take it.

'It's Italy calling,' Bev said before hanging up.

There was a moment's delay before a man's voice came on the line. 'Is Mr Wild there, please?' His accent wasn't Italian, Mia noticed. More like English...no, not English, Australian. 'It's Nathan Royce here.'

Mia felt herself swaying, and clutched the edge of the desk to steady herself as the blood ebbed from her cheeks. 'Would you repeat that name, please?'

'It's *Nathan Royce* here. Mario Carreto's son-in-law. I want to speak to Mr Wild, please. It's about our proposed partnership.'

'Y-yes, Mr Royce. One moment, please.' It couldn't be. It just couldn't! She held the receiver out to Bram, who frowned slightly as he took it from her. He must be wondering... 'It's a—a Mr Royce,' she said huskily.

Bram kept his eye on her as he spoke for several long minutes to Nathan Royce. Mia was only dimly aware of what he was saying. Fragments flitted through her consciousness... 'That sounds most satisfactory... There's just one other thing that needs thrashing out... In a week or so I'll have all the relevant papers drawn up... then I'll fly over and we can sign the documents... Yes, I'm looking forward to meeting you again.'

There couldn't be two Nathan Royces, Mia thought dazedly. Not two Australian Nathan Royces, living in Italy...

She heard a click, and felt Bram's hand on her arm.

'Mia, is there something wrong?'

His touch jolted her senses, bringing a rush of blood back into her face. She swallowed.

'No... nothing. What makes you think that?' How could she tell him? She couldn't! Not after what he had said last night about her taking after her father. How gratified he'd be—how he'd crow—if he learnt that the footloose Nathan Royce, and not the steadfast Martin James, was her real father! Besides, how *could* she say anything? Bram *knew* him. He would demand to know everything, the whole sordid story. He might insist on telling her father about her. She couldn't cope with any of that just now... she had to think!

'I—I wasn't expecting to hear an Australian voice when Italy came on the line,' she hedged. 'You—you're going into some kind of... partnership?'

Bram leaned back in his chair, tapping his chin with one finger. 'Yes, didn't I tell you? We're going to be joint partners in a corn mill in Tuscany, near Florence. The mill belongs to the Carreto family, but Mario, the father, is too old now to run the business single-handedly, and he's passed the reins over to his son-in-law, Nathan Royce.'

But... Mia looked confused, a memory stirring inside her. Her father was an artist, not a businessman. It must be a different Nathan Royce after all. It had to be. It was an incredible coincidence, both men having the same name, and both living in Italy.

'Why do they want a partner?' she asked. 'An *Australian* partner?'

'Nathan has other interests besides the mill. He and his wife are both artists . . . talented painters. I won't go into all the whys and wherefores now, but it suits the family to bring in an overseas partner. And it suits us to have a mill in Europe. It'll be beneficial to both sides.'

Mia's throat constricted. It had to be him! Her father was an artist, and so was the woman he had married after divorcing Mia's mother. Her mother had alluded to it now and then in her bitter moments.

'In a couple of weeks I'll need to fly over there to sign the papers,' Bram said. He was watching her through half-closed lids, and it was only with a supreme effort that she was able to act as though they were discussing nothing more than another business matter. 'If my hand's still in plaster by then you'll have to come with me.'

Her studied calm shattered. 'You mean—to Italy?' She forced the words out. Oh, no, she thought. I couldn't!

He misunderstood her reaction. 'You're *afraid* to go away with me?' he taunted.

She tilted her chin, fighting to control a tangle of conflicting emotions. 'After last night, do you wonder?' Safer, perhaps, to let him believe it was that. She would decide later what to do about . . . Nathan Royce.

He let out his breath in an exasperated sigh. 'I thought I'd made it clear that you are perfectly safe with me. All right, I apologise for last night. I *had* been drinking, and you were . . . well, that wisp of a thing you were wearing did . . . Damn it, Mia, do I have to go down on my bended knee to you? I've said I'm sorry! I was simply making a point. And got a bit carried away. It won't happen again.'

'Good.' Then why didn't she *feel* good? Why did his assurance make her feel so... forlorn? Because he had been more successful than he knew in making his point? Because he had finally made her wake up to the fact that she wanted more from life, more from *love*, than Richard was offering her? But what precisely *did* she want? Why did she feel so confused?

'I want you to take some notes and then type them up for me.' Bram's tone was abrupt now, impatient. 'Bev's busy on something else—I'll have a typewriter brought in here for you. Get on to it quickly, will you? I need to have all the facts at my fingertips when I see the Premier tomorrow.'

'Yes, Mr Wild.'

They worked late, long after everyone else had gone home. Mia's mind began to wander as she typed up the notes she had jotted down earlier. She was trying to picture her father's face, but she couldn't. She had been too young when he'd walked out on them to remember it, and her mother had since removed all the photographs she had had of him, even their wedding photos. Richard's face swam into the void, and she sighed. What was she going to do about Richard? How could she go ahead with their wedding plans, feeling the way she did, feeling so confused, so uncertain? She wasn't being fair to him.

Or to herself. What *did* she want? More than Richard was offering her, certainly.

Her mother would tell her she was chasing after rainbows. Was she? Was it Bram's kisses—or, more particularly, her own reaction to them—that had put this restlessness, these doubts, into her mind? Her mouth twisted. Bram had been right about one thing. He had made her feel things that she never felt when Richard kissed her. With Richard she had never felt anything but warm and contented and secure. Bram's kisses made her ache with a painful sensation she couldn't identify, and the burning ache still smouldered inside her, hurting and bewildering her.

But how could she trust a moment of passion, a moment of...of lust? Even Richard himself had admitted that Bram was a man who could cast a spell over a woman. He was that kind of man. Charming, mesmerising, but unable and unwilling to form and sustain a relationship. She would be mad to let a man like that influence her—a man who had forgotten how to love, who took his pleasure where he could find it, and then callously moved on. She wasn't looking for that kind of love, where passion flared, but wasn't durable, didn't last. She wanted to be the centre of the universe for some man, to feel ecstasy in his arms forever, and she wanted *him* to be the centre of her world. Was she foolish to believe that such a love existed?

'Come on.' Bram's voice rumbled in her ear, startling her. 'Let's go and have something to eat. You can finish the typing in the morning. I'm not seeing the Premier until eleven. We'll come in early.'

'But I've nearly finished...' she began, her fingers flying over the keyboard. If she hadn't had to correct so many careless mistakes, through not concentrating properly, she would have been finished by now!

'You've been typing long enough. When you're tired you make mistakes.' His tone was stern, implacable. 'Stop now!'

She sighed, and turned off the machine. Had he noticed that she had been making mistakes?

He commanded her to drive his car to the Rocks area, where they had a casual Italian-style meal at a waterfront piazza. He ordered pasta for both of them, and a bottle of Italian wine. Was this some kind of initiation, she wondered, in preparation for the trip ahead? She found herself trembling, and didn't know whether it was the thought of flying all the way to Italy with Bram Wild or the prospect of coming face to face with her father that was the cause.

It was an uncomfortably warm, humid evening, unseasonably warm for that time of year, and brooding clouds were gathering overhead, blurring the pearly glow of the swollen moon. The atmosphere seemed to suit her mood. Her raging thoughts were as dark and troubled as the night.

'Want to talk about it, Mia?' Bram asked, and she jumped at the sound of his voice. She raised her eyes to find him watching her, his eyes dark and unfathomable, neither encouraging nor discouraging.

She shook her head. How could she talk about it, when she hadn't resolved anything in her own mind? And Bram Wild would be the last man in the world to help her resolve her dilemma!

'I know what you need,' said Bram, scraping back his chair. 'Come on, let's go.'

'Go where?'

'Home.'

A flicker of apprehension shot through her. Home...to do what? She gave herself a tiny shake. No, he wouldn't dare. Not after last night! He intended to bundle her off to bed—that was what he meant. He thought she was in need of a good night's sleep!

But that wasn't what he had in mind, though he kept her in the dark until they arrived back at his place, having barely spoken to her on the way home, instead flooding the interior of the car with the soothing music of a haunting classical guitar. And it did help. By the time they reached his house she felt a good deal calmer.

'Now,' he said, in that decisive, implacable way of his, 'go upstairs and change. You're going for a swim.'

'Oh!'

'Well, don't just stand there. You brought a swimsuit with you, didn't you? Not that it would matter if you didn't. The pool's quite secluded.'

She flushed scarlet. 'I'll go up and change,' she said huskily. A swim sounded like a great idea. Especially in this oppressive humidity. It might help to wash her brain clear.

'Good. I'd join you if it weren't for this blasted plaster. But I'll come and watch you if you're scared of the dark.'

She paused, almost tripping over the bottom stair. 'I'm not scared of the dark.' Then why was she trembling all over?

'Just of me...mm?' A devilish glint danced in his eyes.

'No!'

'Well, you're sure as hell scared of something. You're a bundle of nerves.'

If I am, she thought, it's largely your fault! 'Would you please leave me alone?' she gasped.

'If that's what you want.'

'It is.'

She ran up to her room. And to show him that she wasn't scared of him—of him or of the dark—she changed into her bathing costume, a sleek black one-piece affair that moulded her slim body like a second

skin, grabbed a towel, and hurried back down the stairs
before she could change her mind.

Her steps faltered as she approached the pool and saw
Bram sprawled in a banana-shaped lounger, talking into
his mobile phone. Damn him! He'd agreed to leave her
alone! Well, she couldn't turn back now. She wouldn't
give him the satisfaction!

He had switched on the pool lights, and she felt agon-
isingly exposed as she walked to the edge of the pool,
dropped her towel, and braced herself to dive in. Why
had he come? Was he testing her courage? Or was he
deliberately trying to unnerve her, to send her scurrying
for cover, because he feared that his kisses might have
given her the wrong impression, the crazy idea that he
was seriously interested in her?

Well, he could set his mind to rest on that score. She
wasn't so stupid as to believe that! And as for his effect
on *her*, well, difficult as it might be, somehow she would
have to show him that his kisses hadn't meant a
thing... that she was immune to him!

With all the will-power she could summon, she re-
mained poised for a moment longer at the edge of the
pool, knowing she was in full view of him, and knowing
that he would be watching her with those taunting, all-
seeing eyes of his. She was damned if she was going to
panic and leap into the pool like a frightened schoolgirl!

She threw her arms out in front of her and executed
a perfect dive into the blue-tinged water. With leisurely
strokes she swam several lengths of the pool, revelling
in the feel of the cool water sliding along her body and
through her hair.

She risked a sideways glance, and saw that Bram was
still talking on the phone, but his eyes were very defi-
nitely still on her. She quickly averted her gaze and rolled

over on to her back, kicking her way to the edge of the pool, enjoying the sensation of the cool water streaming over the contours of her body like the brush of feathery, erotic fingers.

Finally she climbed out of the pool, squeezed the water from her hair, and reached for her towel. She heard a click and knew that Bram had brought his call to an end.

'That feel better?'

'It was great.' She had stopped trembling, she realised thankfully. The dip had done her good.

Bram threw his legs over the side of the lounger and unfolded his lithe frame, falling into step beside her as she headed back to the house.

'You haven't forgotten that we're going to the Blue Mountains for Easter?' he reminded her.

She felt her stomach roll over. 'Your sister is back from her overseas trip?' The question leapt out.

'No, not yet. They don't get back for another fortnight. Oh, don't look so stricken, Mia. You won't be the only woman there. And I won't be the only man. Russ and his wife and two boys are coming. And Bev Loft and her husband. And a few others.'

She felt herself flushing. 'There's room for all of us at your sister's place?'

'More than enough room. It's a guest-house. My sister's in-laws are running it while my sister and her family are away. You'll need to bring plenty of bush-walking gear. And sturdy walking shoes. And something to wear in the evenings. There's golf and tennis too, if you're interested.'

She gulped in a breath of relief. It was beginning to sound like a fun weekend.

It was only when they parted ways at the foot of the stairs that Mia remembered the dilemma that she was going to have to face sooner or later. What to do about Richard.

And, for that matter, what to do about Nathan Royce, the father she might soon have to meet face to face. The father who had never wanted anything to do with her.

CHAPTER SEVEN

THERE was a violent electrical storm overnight, with torrential rain, and it was still raining the next morning, making the atmosphere, if anything, even muggier and more oppressive. As Mia was preparing to go down to breakfast she received a phone call. It was Richard.

'Mia, can I see you tonight? We're leaving tomorrow on this tour.'

She took a deep breath. 'Ric, I want to see you too. But don't you have choir practice tonight?'

'They've given us the night off. To pack and so forth.'

'I'll ask Bram if he needs me.'

'I've got to see you, Mia. Even if it's only for a few minutes.'

She was surprised at the urgency in his voice. It was unlike Richard to be so impatient to see her. Perhaps he cared for her more deeply than she'd thought. She bit her lip, hoping that wouldn't make what she had decided to do more difficult. She swallowed. 'Me too. I'll get back to you.'

I've got to do it. Now, tonight, she thought. I can't let it go on. It's not fair to Richard.

When she came down to breakfast Bram was already dressed for work, as she was too, his head bent over one of the morning newspapers.

'Good morning,' she said as she sat down. She was acutely aware of the erratic beating of her heart.

'Good morning.' Under the flicker of his eyelids she caught a flash of blue, before his lashes swept down again.

She thrust out her chin. 'Bram, do you mind if I have some time off this evening?' She spoke forcefully, making it more than just a request. 'I'd like to go and see Richard. He'll be going away tomorrow.'

'Ah, yes. With his choir.' Bram lowered his newspaper, and now the look he gave her was steady, speculative. 'Go ahead. I thought I'd go to the gym tonight. Since I can't play tennis and I can't go swimming, I need to find some other way to keep fit during the week. You can drop me off on your way.' He paused, his eyes lazily seductive under the thick devil's brows. 'If you want to stay out overnight I'll catch a cab home.'

'I won't,' she said quickly. Too quickly. She had fallen into his trap. And now he was laughing at her. She could see it in the sudden gleam in his eyes, enhancing the intense blue. She felt like kicking herself—or him!

'Then I'll stay at the gym until you're ready to come for me.' His expression was inscrutable as he went back to his newspaper.

'All right.'

She found it hard to concentrate all day. But the time passed reasonably quickly, because it was another busy day. She finished typing up Bram's notes before driving him to the state parliament house offices, where she sat in on Bram's meeting with the Premier, taking notes, which she typed up for Bram during the afternoon.

When she finally dropped Bram off at the gym after a light tuna and salad dinner prepared by Mrs Tibbits, his parting 'Good luck' brought her eyes swiftly to his face. Had he guessed what she was about to do? She glared after him as he swung away. Well, I suppose you're satisfied now, she thought. Arrogant brute! But inside she was aflutter with apprehension. Was she making herself more vulnerable by casting herself adrift from Richard at this particular point of time? With no ring on her finger, would Bram Wild see her as fair game? But it wouldn't be right, it wouldn't be fair to Richard to let the engagement drag on until she had finished working for Bram. Not now that she had made up her mind.

She took a deep breath as she parked the BMW in the underground car park below the block of flats where Richard lived, and mounted the stairs to his apartment. Would he beg her to reconsider? Plead for more time? What if he requested a trial separation rather than a clean break, and begged her to go on wearing his ring for the duration? The ring would be some protection at least...and Bram would never need to know.

'Come in,' said Richard. He seemed nervous, more serious than usual as he stood back to let her past. And he had forgotten to kiss her.

They stood facing each other in silence for an awkward moment, and then, as she opened her mouth to speak, Richard said with a rush, a tinge of regret in his voice, 'It's not working—is it, Mia? You and me.'

Her eyes widened, surprise riffling through her. Had he felt it too? She looked down, shaking her head. 'I'm sorry, Ric.'

'I've been thinking about it all the week,' he said, and heaved a sigh. 'I think it might be best if we...if we called a halt now. It's not going to get any better. Is it?'

'I don't think so.' He wasn't even going to put up a fight. He wasn't even going to ask for a trial separation. He didn't feel any more strongly about her than she did about him. Why had it taken her so long to realise it?

She slipped his ring off her finger and handed it to him. 'You've been a wonderful...friend, Ric,' she said, and she meant it. But a lover? A husband? No. Not for *her*.

'You've been wonderful too. Want me to come with you when you tell your mother?' It was a guarded offer, and she didn't blame him. Her mother would be beside herself! She had thought her daughter was nicely settled and secure. As settled and secure as *she* had been with Martin James.

'Thanks, but no. I'll tell her.'

'I'll tell my parents,' Richard offered.

The doorbell shrilled. Richard's head spun round, a flush sweeping over his face.

'I wonder who that can be?' he said, looking rather like a schoolboy caught smoking behind the school shed. After a moment's hesitation, he hurried to the door.

It was Jenny, his dumpy little friend from the choir. 'Oh, sorry, I didn't know you were here,' Jenny said when she saw Mia. The way she gazed at Richard when she turned to face him was illuminating. Her eyes, wide and shining behind her thick spectacles, were really quite beautiful, it struck Mia. And they were shining for Richard!

'I'd better go,' she said hastily. 'Good luck with the tour, both of you. And...all the best.' Her look encompassed both of them. Why didn't she feel more pain? Some jealousy? All she felt was...a strange kind of melancholy.

No...that wasn't all she felt, she realised as she drove to her mother's. She felt as if a weight had been lifted from her. And along with it had gone the doubts, the turmoil, the confusion of the past days. She felt free!

* * *

As she drove Bram home from the gym, his sharp eyes noticed that she was no longer wearing her engagement ring.

'So you've finally made the break.' An impassive statement of fact. She was surprised there was no gloating, no mockery. He sounded...indifferent. As if he didn't care one way or the other.

Keeping her eyes on the road in front, she said steadily, 'Richard wanted it too. So I guess you were right. We weren't meant for each other. I suppose you're satisfied now.'

'Satisfied? Why should I be? It doesn't affect me one way or the other. I was only thinking of you.' His tone was cold now, remote. 'But I commend you. You've done the right thing. You've told your mother?'

'Yes.' Her mother's reaction had been predictable— and unsympathetic. She had despaired of her 'impossible' daughter ever finding another husband as reliable or as devoted as Richard, and had accused Mia of being as flighty and as unstable as her father. Mia had had to bite her tongue to stop herself retorting, 'Then my father and I should have a lot in common when I meet him in Italy in a week or so!' Only her consideration for her mother's feelings kept her silent. Let her mother recover from this shock first.

'Good.' Bram lapsed into a stony silence. A silence she didn't attempt to break. He seemed to have put up a wall between them. And she knew why. He was showing her, in case she harboured any foolish ideas, that *he* wouldn't be languishing after her, despite the fact that she was now free...that he had only ever kissed her to make her wake up to herself, or to make some point. Never because he had felt anything special for her. She'd known that all along, and yet—it hurt. She wasn't sure why. He didn't have to be so—so *brutal* about it. He was quite safe!

The next morning, Mia was in Bram's office doing some filing when she overheard him making a phone call.

'Samantha? Bram Wild. How are you? I'm fine. How about joining me for lunch? We could talk over that legal matter you were checking out for me. Fine...'

An hour later he left the office with a curt, 'I'm going out to lunch, Mia. I'm being picked up, so you won't need to take me.'

The door banged behind him, and Mia heaved a sigh. He had been brisk and cool with her all morning. Who was Samantha? she wondered. His lawyer? Or more than that? Maybe an old flame, or...a prospective conquest?

She gave herself a tiny shake. Why should she care? She *didn't* care!

She had lunch with Bev Loft at the café next door.

'I'm really looking forward to Easter—aren't you?' said Bev, biting into an egg and lettuce sandwich. 'Peter and I jumped at the invitation when Bram offered. He might work his staff to death, but he's generous and appreciative too. Last year he sent Peter and me to Hawaii...all expenses paid.'

'Oh.' So that was what Bev had meant by 'rewards'. Mia's eyes were thoughtful as she sipped her iced coffee. She had misjudged him—both of them. Maybe Bram wasn't the lady-killer people made him out to be.

And maybe he was.

Who are you trying to fool? an inner voice taunted. Where is he now? With a woman!

Bram kept her at arm's length, the wall firmly, coldly between them right up until he closed the office for Easter at the end of the week. They set off for the Blue Mountains after lunch on Good Friday, Bram only relaxing and becoming more human after they had picked up a passenger on their way. A statuesque brunette, all poise and polish, introduced to her as Samantha Gordon.

The same Samantha he had met for lunch the other day?

'You're not going to make me sit in the back seat on my own, are you, darling?' Samantha fluttered her long eyelashes—they *have* to be false, Mia thought uncharitably—as Bram opened the rear door for her.

'Never,' Bram said, flashing her a smile. The kind of smile a woman might die for, Mia mused idiotically, if she was on the receiving end. 'You'll have Amelia sitting with you in a few moments,' he said. 'I offered her a lift too.'

'Amelia *Lessing*?' Samantha's tapered brows rose.

'Yes. I was aware you knew each other. So I offered her a lift too.'

Mia put her foot down rather too hard as she swung the car away from the kerb. Bram was bringing *two* of his girlfriends? What sort of Bluebeard was he?

Bram directed her to a block of luxury apartments, where Amelia was waiting at the kerb with her Louis Vuitton luggage. She looked as if she could have been a model, or a film star, but it transpired that she was in public relations. And the smooth and sophisticated Samantha, Mia learned, was employed by the legal firm which handled Bram's business. She wondered with a wry smile why she had ever had qualms about this weekend. As if Bram Wild—even if he should deign to lower the guard he had erected against her—would bother making a pass at an innocent young virgin when he had these two delectable sirens panting for his favours!

* * *

'Come on, Mia, now you can dance with me.'

It was almost midnight on Easter Sunday, and this was the first time in three days that Bram had singled her out, the first time that they had come into direct physical contact. It's only a dance, Mia told herself crossly, trying to still the rapid beating of her heart. He's already danced with Samantha and Amelia and Bev Loft and Russ's wife Helen. He *has* to ask you, or it will look as if he's avoiding you. Which he hasn't been, really. He's treated you the same as everyone else. Even Samantha and Amelia haven't had any special treatment. And they've hated it, she suspected with a quick flare of amusement.

Her amusement died when Bram took her into his arms. Why was it, she thought despairingly as she felt her body melting against his, that he only had to touch her to turn every nerve-end to singing fire?

Did he feel it? Dear heaven, she hoped not!

'Enjoying yourself?' he asked as their bodies swayed in unison to a lilting love-song drifting from the compact-disc player. She realised the song was 'Love is lovelier the second time around', and the thought popped into her head that Bram might have chosen it deliberately to cheer her up after her break-up with Richard, to remind her that there was always another chance for her. Not that he would share such a sentiment himself. Bram no longer believed in love. Or marriage. Or any of the things she still believed in, despite her experience with Richard.

She glanced up at him, trying not to think about the strong warm hand that was enclosing hers, or be affected by the erotic pressure of his plaster cast as it brushed against her spine, or be too aware of his warm breath on her cheek. Somehow she managed to find her voice.

'It's been fun,' she said, and it had. The bush walks, in particular. The bushland surrounding the guest-house was magical. She had been overcome by the staggering splendour of the rugged sandstone ridges, the steep gorges, and the jungle-like forests stretching as far as the eye could see. The mountain air was unbelievably crisp and clear after the close, humid air of the city and she had greedily gulped it in as they had gone on their strenuous bush walks and picnicked in ferny gullies, and as they had drunk in the exhilarating views from a number of look-outs. And the Blue Mountains were truly blue, she had been delighted to discover, the brilliant blue haze hanging around the mountains contrasting with the deeply saturated ochres and yellows of the precipitous sandstone cliffs and the deeply eroded canyons.

'You might be small, but you're a game little thing.' Bram's tone, though teasing, was more admiring than patronising. 'It's been an education watching you battling through the bush, scrambling over rocks, tramping your little legs off. All without a word of complaint.'

He had been *watching* her? She almost missed her step, and felt a sudden clamminess in her fingers, a clamminess she hoped he couldn't feel too. What would he think if he did?

'It's all been too much for Sam and Amelia, I fear.' A wry smile deepened the creases in his cheeks, and Mia felt an answering smile tugging at her lips. After the first day's strenuous bush walk, both Amelia and Samantha had elected to stay behind on subsequent forays into the bush and play golf or tennis instead, and the only other single male guest beside Bram, a recently divorced business friend of his, called Tom, had chosen to stay with them.

Mia wondered if Bram would have stayed behind and played golf with them if he hadn't had his arm in plaster.

She had seen more of him than she had expected to, but there were always others present, and he had treated her the same as everyone else, neither shunning her nor giving her any special attention. Until now. And even this couldn't be termed 'special' attention, Mia reflected pensively, because he had already given the same attention to each of the other female guests first!

The long homestead-style veranda was an ideal place to dance, romantically lit as it was by a string of coloured lights and the brilliant glow of the full moon. The buzz of cicadas and the sharp little chirps of the night birds, or possibly bats, rising from the surrounding bush only added to the heady atmosphere.

This was the first night that Bram had suggested dancing. On the two previous nights they had all lingered over dinner until it was time to retire, with the exception of Russ's two boys, who had been packed off early to bed. The conversation at dinner each evening had been lively and wide-ranging, and Bram had made sure that everyone swapped places often to mix them all up. If he had made any nocturnal visits after retiring, Mia was unaware of it—and didn't want to know!

Russ and his family left for home early on Easter Monday morning, but the others didn't plan to leave until the afternoon. At breakfast, Bram suggested a last trek through the bush before lunch. This time Samantha decided to join them. Amelia wavered for a moment, but finally opted to stay behind with Tom and play golf.

Samantha stayed close to Bram all the way down the steep timbered slope, often clinging to his arm for support and stumbling over rocks in her high-heeled de-

signer boots. Mia pushed on ahead, following the path
Bram had chosen, which he said led to the foot of a
waterfall. Bev and her husband Peter were close behind
her until Bev got a pebble in her shoe and sank down
on to a rock to shake it out, at the same time seizing the
chance for a breather.

Not realising that they were no longer following
behind, Mia kept on scrambling down the slope until
she came to a bubbling brook. She saw a path on the
other side, and jumped across, keeping to what she
thought was the same path until she saw others criss-
crossing it, and became confused. She paused, expecting
to see the others following behind. When they didn't
appear, she bit her lip, wondering what to do. Which
was the path she had followed here? She couldn't be
sure. Somewhere near by she could hear the roar of a
waterfall, and, knowing that that was where they were
heading, she made a quick decision, chose the most likely
path, and made her way towards the sound—only to find
herself getting deeper and deeper into the bush. And then
the path petered out altogether, and there was nothing
ahead but a jungle of impenetrable trees and scrub.

She swung round, her heartbeat quickening in sudden
fear. She still couldn't hear the others behind her. The
only sounds she could hear were bush sounds and the
roar of the nearby waterfall. When she called out Bram's
name there was no answer.

Fighting down an upsurge of panic, she headed back
the way she had come, calling out every now and then
as she pushed her way through the encroaching scrub.

She came across the criss-crossing paths. But which
was the one she had followed here in the first place?

She had no idea! If she chose the wrong one she could
find herself wandering even deeper into the bush, where

she might never be found. She tried to remember the safety precautions Bram had told them the first day: If you get lost, stay put...don't wander about. But the thought of staying put was terrifying! What if no one thought of looking *here*?

She thought of climbing a tree to see if she could see anything from there, but after a quick look round she dismissed the idea. The trees—gums, wattles, tea-trees, thrusting from a tangle of scrubby bushes—were all too spindly, or too bushy.

She started shouting again, at the top of her lungs. 'Coo-ee! Coo-ee! Bram! Bram!' She knew her shouts wouldn't carry far, but she kept on just the same. 'Coo-ee! Bram! He-elp!'

Just when she was starting to despair she heard an answering call.

'Coo-ee!'

Her heart leapt to her throat. Was it a bird? Or was it...?

'I'm here!' she yelled frantically. 'Coo-ee! Bram! Bram! I'm here!'

'Mia!'

She felt a choking sensation. It was Bram's voice!

'Mia, I'm coming! Keep shouting!'

'Bram! Bram!' Her shouts exultant now, she guided him to her, catching her breath as she heard what sounded like a stampeding animal thrashing its way through the bush. And then Bram burst into view—the most welcome sight she had seen in her life!

With a sob of relief, she flung herself at him and threw her arms around his neck, gasping as she clung to him, 'Oh, Bram, I knew you'd find me!' Only to be silenced as his arms caught her round the waist and swept her into the air, his mouth frantically showering her with kisses—her lips, her eyes, her cheeks, her throat—as if he was as relieved as she.

When he finally set her back on her feet she was breathless, overwhelmed by the sensations running riot inside her.

'What possessed you to go wandering off on your own?' He fired the question at her but, for all its harshness, there was a faint tremor in his voice.

'I'm sorry,' she whispered. She must have given him a fright. Not because she was in any way special to him, but because he felt responsible for her, as he would for any of his guests. 'I didn't realise, at first, that I had... When I did it was too late. I was lost. I...stayed put. As you said.'

'Thank goodness you did. If you'd panicked you could have ended up anywhere.'

She risked a glance up at his face, and gave a tiny cry. 'Bram, your face is all scratched! And there's a cut on your——'

'They're nothing,' he cut in, grabbing her arm as if she might run off and disappear again if he didn't. 'Let's get back to the others. I ordered them to stay by that brook. It's time we were heading back for lunch.'

'I'm sorry,' she said again, the fringe of her lashes casting shadows on her cheek. 'I've made you miss the waterfall.'

'Never mind.' His voice was hard now, distant. He was putting up that wall again between them. Now that he was over his relief at finding her, was he regretting those feverish kisses a moment ago? Of course he was! *They* couldn't be explained away as a cold-blooded demonstration. Or to make a point. They had been thoroughly spontaneous.

She brushed her hair back from her face. Not that that meant anything. He'd been worried, that was all. He had kissed her in the heat of the moment, from relief. By the time they got back he'd have forgotten all about it. But would *she* ever forget?

While Bram was packing their bags into the boot of his BMW, Amelia and Samantha, already impatiently waiting in the back seat, started discussing the weekend as if Mia, sitting in front of them in the driver's seat, didn't exist. Or didn't matter.

'I'll be glad to get home,' Amelia complained. 'It was nothing like I was expecting. You'd think a weekend with Bram Wild would have had a *bit* of glamour and glitz. He didn't even take us to a decent restaurant for dinner.'

'Oh, I didn't mind the guest-house meals so much,' Samantha answered with a sigh. 'It was those wretched bush walks. He'd made them sound as if they were going to be such fun. Fun! Ha! And as for this morning's débâcle...' She dropped her voice, but not so low that Mia couldn't still hear. 'When he went charging off after *you know who*, leaving me to the mercy of—well, there could have been snakes or lizards or wild animals or anything, it was the last straw!'

'And he couldn't even play golf or tennis with us,' Amelia commiserated. 'He's changed since he broke that hand of his. He's nowhere near as much fun any more. He turns down invitations right and left.'

'I know. I got quite a shock when he asked me out to lunch the other day. And when he asked me up here for the weekend. I hadn't seen him for ages.'

'He only asked you at the last minute too?' Amelia sounded surprised. 'If you knew the invitations I turned

down to come up here! Tom, I guess, was some consolation. But he's not——'

'Shh. Here he comes.'

Mia hid a smile as Bram slid into the seat beside her.
Poor Amelia. Poor Samantha. Surely Bram could have
guessed they'd hate this kind of weekend? Why had he
asked them? And why only at the last minute?

Her hands tightened on the wheel. Because, if he
hadn't, *she* would have been the only single woman. And
she might have been silly enough to get the idea that he
was singling her out! And he wouldn't want that. Oh,
no. She'd be a fool not to have noticed how wary and
distant he had become since she had broken off her
engagement to Richard.

Well, you needn't worry, Bram Wild... She sucked
in an angry breath. I'm well aware you no longer believe
in love or marriage. I'm well aware that you'll never give
your heart to another woman—let alone an unsophisticated *virgin*. You didn't have to go to those lengths to
keep me at bay. I wouldn't touch you with a ten-foot
barge-pole. Not if you were the last man on earth!

'Is your passport up to date?'

Mia looked up from her notepad, her pen poised. 'I
think so.'

'Make sure. I want to book our flight to Rome. For
some time next week. All the paperwork will be ready
by then.'

Next week! Her stomach clenched. Within days, she
and her father could well come face to face! What was
she going to do when she saw him? Tell him who she
was? But what if he rejected her again, the way he had
rejected her twenty-odd years ago? How could she bear
it?

Bram was eyeing her quizzically. 'You'll love Tuscany,' he said. 'And the Royces will welcome you with open arms. They'll make you feel like a long-lost daughter.'

Her eyes dilated. Long-lost daughter! Why had he said that? Did he *know*? She fought for control. No...how could he? It was just a throw-away phrase. It was rather funny really. If he only knew what he'd said! She choked back a giggle, slightly edged with hysteria.

'May I share the joke?'

She sobered instantly, shaking her head. 'It's nothing.' She bit her lip, suddenly greedy to learn more about the father she had never known...or had been too young to remember. 'Mr Royce is an Australian, you said?'

'Yes. But he's been living in Italy for about twenty years. I understand he's only been back to Australia once in that time—when he came out here last year.'

She felt the room tilt, and was glad she was sitting down. Her father had come back to Australia last year, and hadn't bothered to look her up? She felt a wave of hurt, of renewed bitterness. Her mother had always said he didn't care about her, and now she knew it was true.

'How long was he here?' Her voice sounded strange to her own ears, as if it belonged to somebody else.

'Long enough to look over my operations and to exhibit some of his paintings. And his wife's.'

'His wife came with him?' She knew Bram was looking at her oddly, but she couldn't hold the questions back.

'They're never apart.'

Mia swallowed. Was that why her father hadn't contacted her? Because his wife had been with him, and she was unaware that he had a daughter by a previous marriage?

'Do they have any children?' She tried to make it sound like simple curiosity, but she was barely breathing as she asked.

'Two boys and a girl, from memory.'

Shock riffled through her. She had two half-brothers and a half-sister she had never known existed! No wonder her father didn't care about her. He had replaced her the same way that he had replaced his wife. But... Her eyes grew pensive. Did he never wonder about his first-born child?

'Nathan, in a lot of ways, is more Italian than the Italians,' Bram drawled. 'Not that he looks Italian. He has ginger hair. And blue eyes. No, not blue... green. That's right... grey-green.' He was looking into *her* eyes as he spoke, and there was a probing query in the blue depths. And then his gaze flicked over her hair. She realised she had stopped breathing.

'Mia...what is Nathan Royce to you?' The sharp blue eyes impaled hers, too perceptive for comfort.

The question echoed into the silence. She sat as if carved from stone, staring wordlessly at him. She would have to tell him. Even if it meant putting up with his taunts. She took a deep quivering breath.

'He's my father. Martin James was my *stepfather*.' Even as she braced herself for Bram's reaction she felt a rush of relief that it was out at last.

'I see.' She could see his mind ticking over. Any minute now he would say 'I knew there was something about you that didn't add up...'

But he surprised her. 'Poor Mia. So you have lost not one, but two fathers.'

She had been expecting anything but sympathy and understanding from Bram Wild. She closed her eyes against the prick of sudden tears.

'He was never a father to me,' she said in a muffled voice. 'He walked out when I was only two years old. I don't even remember him...' And then she added with a rush, 'He only married my mother because she was p-pregnant, and because he was forced into it!'

'You really think a man can be forced into marriage? Give the man credit, Mia, for at least trying to make a go of it.'

'He didn't try very hard—or for very long.'

'So bitter! And now you intend to turn your back on him, the way he turned his back on you... is that it?'

'No! I don't know! My mother...' She dashed a tear from her eye. Her mother would urge her to let it lie...she would say he didn't deserve a second chance, that he wasn't worth it, that he wouldn't want her intruding on his new life anyway, and she would only end up hurt.

'Think about what *you* want, Mia, not what your mother would want.'

She shook her head, too choked up to speak. Silent tears began to roll down her cheeks.

In a fluid movement, Bram came round from behind his desk and took her pen and notepad from her fingers, and dropped them on to his desk. Then, with his good hand, he drew her to her feet.

'Why don't you let it all out, Mia? Have a good cry.'

She felt his arms close around her and she didn't resist. No matter what happened afterwards, she needed this moment... she needed the comfort he was offering—all the more valuable because it was so rare, so unexpected. She nestled her face in his shoulder and let the tears flow... tears for herself, for her father, for what she had lost... tears she had been holding back for as long as she could remember.

'That's right, Mia...' Bram's voice was a soothing rumble above her right ear, and she wondered dimly how she had ever thought of him as hard and unfeeling. 'You've been bottling up your feelings for far too long. You've never been allowed to cry for the father you lost, have you?'

She shook her head, and gulped, 'I...I'm sorry...'

'You should learn not to feel guilty, Mia, about having feelings...powerful passions...needs of your own. You've spent far too long trying to be what others want you to be...what Richard wants...what your mother wants. It's *your* life, Mia. Start thinking about what you want for a change. Do what *you* want to do.'

She looked up at him, tears blurring her eyes and glistening on her lashes. She knew one thing she wanted. 'I want to meet my father,' she said.

Bram's gaze held hers for a long moment, and she saw something kindling in the blue depths, a look she couldn't define. But it was enough to send a quiver through her. And in that moment she knew there was something else she wanted. But that would be far more difficult, if not impossible, to attain.

CHAPTER EIGHT

'I WANT you to take the rest of the afternoon off,' Bram said. 'Go and check that passport. And then pack a bag for two nights. We're going to Melbourne.'

Melbourne again? Mia looked at him enquiringly, trying not to think about Natasha.

'I have meetings there all day tomorrow,' Bram explained. 'And in the evening there's a dinner dance. Russ and Helen usually go to these affairs, but they have a school function to go to, and since we'll be there...' He broke off as the phone rang. 'Yes? Hold the call for a minute, Bev.' He turned back to Mia. 'We'll fly down tonight instead of first thing in the morning. It won't be so rushed. I'll make a booking for dinner. Ever been to Fanny's?'

He intended having dinner with *her* this time? Mia swallowed, and shook her head. And *Fanny's*, of all places! She could imagine him wanting to take Samantha or Amelia to a swanky restaurant like Fanny's, but why would he want to take *her* there? She was only his driver...his temporary personal assistant. Of course, he was used to dining at such places—with a different woman, no doubt, each time. He wouldn't think anything of it. Or care what people thought. She ought to know that by now.

'Why don't you go out and buy a new dress for the dinner dance tomorrow night?' Bram made it sound more like a decree than a question of choice. 'Let your head go, and buy something stunning. I'll bump up your next pay cheque to cover it.'

'That won't be——'

'I want you back here by five,' he barked, cutting off her protest. 'I'll ring Tibby and get her to pack a bag for me. Pick it up before you come.' He turned back to the phone. 'OK, Bev, you can put that call through now.'

Mia stood hesitating a moment, and then headed for the door.

'What beautiful flowers!' she exclaimed, admiring the brilliant display of dahlias, roses and chrysanthemums beside their table. 'Fresh flowers always bring a place a life, don't you think?'

Bram chuckled softly. 'You're refreshing, Mia, you know that? Other women would be looking around to see who was here...there's usually somebody notable dining here. Or they'd be preening themselves, and trying to *be* noticed. *They* would say it's the clientele that brings the place to life.'

She eyed him uncertainly. 'Is that why you brought me here? To be impressed by the clientele?'

'Lord, no. Don't you know me better than that? I thought you might enjoy it—simple as that. The food here is exquisite, and the service is always superb. Having dragged you out on picnics and to country guest-houses and into rough-and-ready cafés and bistros, I thought you might like a bit of elegance for a change. You seem to enjoy new experiences. And I enjoy watching *your* enjoyment.'

'Oh.' She wasn't quite sure how to take that. Was he being patronising? 'There is so much you haven't done, haven't seen!' he had told her once. She frowned into his face, but could see no discernible mockery there. His expression was unfathomable, but one glance was sufficient for the nerves of her stomach to begin an agonising somersault. She looked away quickly.

'Appetiser, madam?' A smooth-haired waiter slipped a plate in front of her. As he drifted away, Mia looked up at Bram with amusement dancing in her eyes.

'Eggs on toast?'

'Quail eggs,' he explained with a smile. That rare, heart-stopping smile! Had any woman lucky enough to see it ever been able to resist it?

Natasha had. She felt her spirits dip. And Bram still held a torch for her, and always would... So don't be silly, Mia. Play with fire and you'll end up burnt.

She bent over her appetiser—a miniature fried egg on a round of crisp fried bread. It was delicious! The food to follow was equally enticing, and beautifully presented, each course accompanied by the best Australian wines. Bram was wining and dining her in style this evening! But were his thoughts with her... or with his lost love, Natasha, who lived somewhere here in Melbourne? Did he secretly wish that it was Natasha sitting opposite him now? Did he dream that one day she would come back to him? Or... had he finally put her out of his mind... for good?

If he had, dared she hope...? Mia, you poor fool, don't even think it! Bram's scars have gone too deep for him to ever trust or love another woman. To think otherwise would be to believe in fairy-tales. And fairy-tales and Bram Wild don't mix. When will you ever learn?

'It's a glorious evening. Let's walk back to the hotel,' Bram said as they rose to leave, and it seemed quite natural when he caught her hand in his at the traffic-lights—and kept hold of it as they strolled on, peering into shop windows on their way, discovering that they both liked looking in bookshops, which led to a lively discussion on the books they had read and others they intended to read. When they reached their hotel Bram didn't have to twist her arm to persuade her to join him for a nightcap in the piano bar, where their conversation spread to the theatre and the arts.

'Have you ever wanted to be an artist, Mia?' Bram asked.

She knew why he was asking. Because he knew that her father, Nathan Royce, was an artist. 'I did once— a long time ago,' she admitted. 'But my mother persuaded me to take up the piano instead.'

'Because she didn't trust artists, and didn't want her daughter getting involved in the wicked art world?' Bram's tone was gentle rather than mocking.

'Something like that.'

'And because you loved your mother and didn't want to hurt her you buried any inclination you had and threw all your pent-up passions into music.'

A flush shadowed her high, delicate cheekbones. She wished he hadn't mentioned passions! 'Not only buried it, but lost it,' she said, trying to make light of it. 'I can't even draw a straight line now.'

'Maybe, if you tried again now…if you had lessons…'

'Maybe.' She gulped, and smiled, surprised—and grateful—that he should care. Nobody else ever had. At her smile, the hard lines of his face gentled further, and what she saw revealed there made her ache so much that she wanted to cry. This man has so much to give, she thought with a rush of concern for *him*. If only he would allow himself to trust again, to love again, to share what he has to offer…

'It's getting late,' Bram said, and she wondered if he was retreating behind his protective wall again. But there was nothing abrasive about his tone, and his expression was still perfectly relaxed. He had certainly changed—mellowed—since she had first come to work for him!

They caught a lift up to their floor, and when they paused outside her room to say goodnight Mia found she was slightly breathless—and it had nothing to do with their walk in the fresh night air earlier! It was the way Bram was looking at her! Apprehension quivered through her. She had seen that look before in other men's eyes...perhaps never in Richard's eyes, but she had seen it in some of her courting friends, and in the eyes of film stars on the screen, on TV...a smouldering hunger. Desire! She felt her throat constricting. What did Bram expect of her... in return for all that wining and dining? Would an avowed womaniser like Bram Wild be content with a polite 'thank you'? Surely, in her case...? After all, she was only his employee, not one of his women...

Then what was she doing just standing there, staring back at him? Say goodnight, Mia, and *go*!

'A man could drown in those eyes of yours,' Bram murmured. The words were accompanied by the merest hint of a smile, so that it was hard to tell if he was serious or just teasing her, just doing a line he'd done a thousand times before.

Go now, Mia, you fool! But she couldn't move. She was sure that, if she tried, her legs would crumple beneath her.

'You're lovely, Mia.'

Her eyes widened and filled with an aching intensity as he lifted a hand and idly brushed his fingers down her cheek. 'No woman's skin is like yours. It doesn't look the same, or feel the same, or have the same delicate, elusive scent.' He traced a finger down a fragile blue vein.

'Don't. Please,' she whispered.

'No…you're right.' His hand dropped to her shoulder. 'It's late. Go and get your beauty sleep, Mia. I'll see you at breakfast.' He swung away from her so abruptly that she had to look away, rummaging in her handbag for her door key to hide the sudden hurt in her eyes. He had remembered in time that she was only his employee. And a virgin, at that! Bram Wild had too many other women to choose from to risk a charge of sexual harassment from an employee! And he had told her he didn't ravish virgins!

But what if the virgin…*wanted* to be ravished?

Bram's meetings kept them both occupied for most of the next day, with only a short break for lunch, when Bram met up with some men from the Wheat Board. Since Mia was going to be sitting in on their afternoon meeting, and the lunch was in their boardroom, she was invited too. And something she overheard at the start of their luncheon sent her heart—foolishly—soaring.

'Good to see you again so soon, Bram,' one of the men said. He added, turning to Mia, 'Bram and I had dinner together the last time he was down in Melbourne. He mentioned that he had brought you with him, but I understand you were visiting an aunt that evening. It's a pleasure to meet you this time.'

'Thank you.' So Bram hadn't had dinner with Natasha that night—or had a clandestine meeting with her! Relief throbbed through her. And at once she mentally chided herself. What a fool she had been ever to have imagined such a thing in the first place. Natasha was a happily married woman, and it was years since she had run out on Bram and married Tim Kennedy-Ford. The experience might have made Bram cynical about love and marriage, but it was ridiculous to imagine that he would still be carrying a torch for her after all this time, still be cherishing some hope of winning her back. He was well aware that Natasha didn't love him and never would. Perhaps he even hated her now for what she had done to him.

'Mm... You look sensational!'

'Thank you.' She had let her head go and bought the sort of dress she had always dreamed of but had never dared to wear when she was going out with Richard, even if she could have afforded the expensive price tag. Richard would have hated it. He disliked anything at all showy or flamboyant, and he shared her mother's notion that redheads should avoid wearing anything red. And this was red! Flaming red. It was strapless, with a nipped-in waist and a short skirt, and with it she wore a floating chiffon scarf and bright red sandals.

'You look rather dashing yourself,' she said, a lump rising in her throat at the understatement. He looked heavenly! This was the first time she had seen him in evening dress, and he wore his white dinner-jacket with the easy grace of a James Bond or a Rhett Butler. The sleeves had been cut wide enough, she noticed, to cover his plaster cast—or most of it. Not that the glimpse at the end of his sleeve in any way detracted from his aura of potent masculinity—it seemed only to enhance it. With his naturally wayward hair and his compelling blue eyes, the whole effect was devastating!

The dinner dance was in the ballroom at the Regent Hotel, where they were staying, and she and Bram found themselves sitting at a table with a handful of Bram's business colleagues—some of whom they had met during the day—and their wives or girlfriends.

It was during the main course—tender medallions of veal in a tomato and thyme sauce—that the evening took a decided down-turn. Mia noticed Bram staring across the crowded ballroom at a couple who were only just arriving. Though his expression was inscrutable as he watched them wend their way to a table near their own, Mia glimpsed a faint tightening of muscle at the edge of his jaw, indicating that he was not as calm as he was trying to make out.

She looked more closely at the couple, at the woman in particular, an exquisite creature in a cloud of pink tulle. Her eyes narrowed as the woman caught Bram's eye and appeared to stumble, her companion coming swiftly to her rescue, catching her arm in his, his gentle grey eyes showing quick concern. Mia's body stiffened in shock. That woman...the pale red-gold hair, the smooth madonna-like hairstyle, the pale skin, the delicate bones...and, above all, her reaction to seeing Bram there...and his reaction at seeing her...

Natasha!

It had to be! But *was* it? Already Bram was turning back to answer a question someone had put to him, giving the person opposite him his full attention, giving no outward indication that he had just come face to face with the woman who had once jilted him—the only woman he had ever loved. But Mia, because she had become so acutely aware of Bram in recent days, sensed that he was not as unmoved as he appeared, only she, perhaps, noticing the tiny muscle clenched at the edge of his jaw, as if he was attempting some form of control.

Yes, she thought, it's Natasha. And Bram still carries a torch for her.

After the meal, the band struck up with a dance medley, and Bram drew Mia to her feet and swung her into his arms. But she knew that his mind was not on the waltz—or on her. She slid a poignant look up at him, her eyes shadowed by her thick lashes, only to drop them just as quickly, jolted by what she saw. He knew! He had seen in her eyes that she knew Natasha was here! Oh, lord, what else had he seen?

You poor fool, Mia, what does it matter what he has seen? As if he cares what you know, or what you're thinking or feeling. You're nothing to him, and if you have any sense he'll be nothing to you. He still loves Natasha. He still wants her.

It seemed inevitable when Bram finally steered her to the table where Natasha and her husband were sitting side by side.

Natasha looked up as they approached, and Mia saw quick apprehension widen the lovely blue eyes. She's afraid he's going to make a scene, Mia thought, translating the look. And, from what I've heard about Bram Wild's temper in the past, he's perfectly capable of making one!

But Bram was all politeness, all control, as he inclined his head and said coolly, 'Natasha. Tim. It's been a long time.'

Natasha's husband Tim, a thin man, slightly thinning on top, rose, after a slight hesitation, to his feet. 'Good evening, Bram. Yes...it has been a long time.'

Bram slipped his good hand round Mia's waist. 'I'd like you to meet a friend of mine...Mia James. Mia...Natasha and Tim Kennedy-Ford.'

'How do you do?' How polite they all were! But what jumbled emotions were simmering underneath? Just what was Bram up to? Mia brooded. And why had he called her a friend, when she was only his driver, his assistant—a mere employee? Did he *look* on her as a friend now? Or had he only said it for Natasha's benefit...to give the impression that she was one of his women? Perhaps even to make Natasha jealous—to impress on her what *she* could have had?

'Would you allow me to dance with your wife?' Bram asked Tim, his tone smoothly impassive. 'For old times' sake?'

Mia felt her heart twist while Tim wavered for a second. But his natural good manners won. 'It's all right with me. It's up to Natasha.'

'Natasha?' Bram's gaze shifted to Tim's wife. Mia couldn't look at him, didn't want to see what might be visible in his eyes.

Natasha rose wordlessly, and Tim turned to Mia. 'May I?'

They all drifted on to the dance-floor together. As Tim slipped his arm round her waist and held her loosely as they fell into step, Mia's eyes drifted, like a moth to a flame, to Bram and Natasha as they swung past, Natasha almost swallowed up in Bram's arms. They were deep in conversation, she noticed, and Natasha's lovely eyes were intent on Bram's face, as his were on hers. There was no anger, no resentment apparent...they seemed utterly absorbed in each other.

Mia felt the earth rock slightly beneath her feet with the shock of the white-hot stab of jealousy that tore through her. She had never experienced such primitive emotion before, and it almost tore her apart with its violence. Even worse was the jolting realisation that what lay behind these charged, desperate feelings was far more than mere jealousy, mere pique, at seeing her escort in the arms of his old love. She knew now, with a blinding certainty, that she was in love with Bram. In love as she had never loved before.

And it was all so hopeless, so futile! Because he was still tied to Natasha, and always would be, even if, after this evening's encounter, he failed to win her back. Natasha would always be the only woman for him . . . he would never allow any other woman to take her place in his heart.

Mia wasn't sure how she got through the rest of the evening, but she managed it by fixing a smile to her lips and calling on resources she had never needed to call on before. And when Bram took her up to her room afterwards she made sure she already had her key in her hand when they reached it, and as she thrust it into the lock, keeping her face carefully averted, she dismissed him with a lightness she was far from feeling. 'Thank you, Bram, for taking me tonight. It was lovely.'

But when she pushed the door open and stepped inside he followed her!

'Let me come in, Mia . . . for just a minute.'

She wheeled round. 'Why?' Apprehension, mingled with anger, sharpened her voice. If he thought he was going to use her as a surrogate Natasha . . . or even try to forget Natasha in her arms, he was very much mistaken!

'What is it, Mia? What's wrong?' His hand reached out and touched her lightly on the shoulder, sending an electrical charge spiking through her body.

'Nothing's wrong.'

'Isn't it? Ever since we met up with Natasha you've been studiously avoiding my eye. Oh, you've smiled and laughed and put on an admirable act, but you forget, Mia . . . I know you pretty well by now.'

Hot prickles broke out all over her skin. But not that well! Not well enough to guess how she felt about him. Please heaven!

'You think I still care for Natasha?' he asked bluntly.

She bit back the obvious answer, and instead, said stiffly, 'That's your own business. It's nothing to do with me.'

'Isn't it?' He put his hand under her chin and tilted it upwards, his eyes boring into her face. 'You wouldn't be jealous, Mia, by any chance?'

She caught her breath. 'Jealous?' She gave a scathing cough of laughter. Which was quite an achievement in the circumstances. 'What right or reason would I have to be jealous? Just because you escorted me tonight I don't expect... I don't imagine...' She snapped the rest off, seizing on anger to cover the pain and the turmoil inside her. 'You're so used to having women fall at your feet, Bram Wild, that you have developed a mightily inflated ego!'

'Let's leave other women out of this. If they want to carry on that way I can't be held responsible. I'm more interested in... what you think and feel, Mia. Because you do feel something... don't you? Much as you try to fight it, you know deep down that it's true...'

Her heart seemed suddenly to seize up in her chest. For a moment she thought she might stop breathing. She dragged in a deep lungful of air, self-preservation bringing a swift, if a trifle husky, 'Your conceit, Bram Wild, is boundless!' If she admitted the truth she would be out of a job, and out of his life, within five seconds. And how could she bear it? Even if she was only putting off the inevitable she couldn't let that happen to her... not *yet*.

'Face the truth, Mia.' His fingers, light as silk, felt the muscles at the back of her neck, tracing the line of tension along her nape. For one wild, erratic moment she thought he was discovering things about her with his fingertips that she would never voluntarily reveal.

'You'd like to believe it!' she growled furiously, but it came out as little more than a croak.

'Yes, I would...' His fingers moved, brushing softly over her cheek and delicately caressing the curl of her ear. She could barely stop herself from gasping.

'Don't Bram...please,' she begged. 'You're not being fair.'

'Deny that you feel something for me, Mia. Go on, look into my eyes and deny it,' he challenged, his eyes searching hers, causing ripples of panic in her stomach.

'No!' She tried to twist her face away, but his fingers raked back through her hair and he held her head tilted up to his.

'Look at me, Mia. Tell me what you see in *my* eyes. You think *I* feel nothing for *you*?'

The extraordinary blue eyes blazed into hers, and she trembled at the tenderness, the smouldering passion she saw in the glowing depths. But was it for her or for...?

'You're still not sure, are you, Mia?' He threaded his fingers through her hair in an oddly caressing gesture. 'Then I'm going to have to show you...'

'No...please!' Her instinctive protest was lost beneath the onslaught of his mouth, and from that moment on she was lost. She found herself actually inviting the hungry invasion of his lips, wanting to savour the sweet torture only he could offer, opening her mouth the instant his lips met hers, submitting willingly, eagerly, to his searching possession.

Of their own volition her hands crept up to entwine themselves round his neck, and her body moved subtly closer to his, exulting in the feel of him. His mouth hardened, grinding over hers, slaking a passionate thirst that matched her own, and it was only when she heard his faintly audible groan that sanity flooded back, and, weak and gasping, she tore her mouth away, uttering a desperate cry.

'I'm not Natasha!'

He held her away from him, staring down at her with passion-drugged eyes. 'No, you're not,' he agreed, and she felt her heart twist. He was saying that no woman would ever mean to him what Natasha had—what she still did. She, Mia, might mean something to him, but she would never have his heart entirely. And she would be a fool to settle for less. Because, whatever he offered her, it wouldn't be enough—not for *her*. And, going by his past record, it wouldn't last long either. And that would be worse than having nothing at all.

'Please leave now, Bram,' she pleaded. She was trembling all over, and the temptation to give in to the erotic feelings still pulsating through her was strong. But she mustn't...she couldn't!

'If that's what you really want,' Bram said, dropping his hand and stepping away from her. 'Perhaps one day, Mia, you'll even...come to *me*. And, when you do, I'll be waiting.'

CHAPTER NINE

MIA sat in her comfortable first-class seat and watched the Sydney Harbour Bridge and the white overlapping shells of the opera house receding from view. It was hard to believe that she was on her way to Italy at last. So much had happened in the past week!

Most of her spare time had been spent preparing for the trip and convincing her mother that she should go. Mia had been frank about the fact that she would be seeing her father—it was only fair that her mother should know. As expected, her mother had been upset at the idea, and had reacted by lashing out at Bram.

'Since you've been working for that man, Mia, you've changed—and I'm not sure I like what's happening to you. You're thrown away a perfectly wonderful husband...'

'Fiancé, Mother.'

That was brushed aside. 'You dress differently, you wear your hair differently, you jet about the country-side... and now you say you're going off to Italy with him.'

'That's my job, Mother.'

'Is it?' Her mother frowned into her face. 'I hope you're not falling for him, Mia. Because you'll only end up badly hurt if you are. From what I've heard about him, Bram Wild is not the type of man who'll ever want to settle down. They say he's an incurable workaholic, far too fond of his jet-setting bachelor lifestyle to ever want to be tied down to a wife and a cosy home-life.

Men of his kind, Mia...they can have any woman they want, any time they want. Marriage is not on their agenda...'

'You don't have to worry, Mother. I know all that.'

Her mother was not convinced. 'Richard says he's dangerously attractive—the type of man who could sweep any woman off her feet. Your father was like that, Mia. He had charm...charisma...I remember how he swept me off *my* feet. I was young, like you, Mia—young and impressionable. And foolish.' Her voice turned bitter. 'I thought I could change him...hold him. But I couldn't. He didn't want marriage...he couldn't wait to get out of it.'

'And yet he did marry again, didn't he?' Mia pointed out quietly. 'And that marriage has lasted for twenty-odd years. Maybe you were both just too young...or not really meant for each other. You married again too, Mother. And you were happy with my...with Martin, weren't you?'

'Yes, I was,' her mother said mistily. 'But that's because I felt secure with him—I knew I could trust him and rely on him. And that's what counts, Mia. Security. Romantic fantasies are for the young and foolish.'

They were back to Bram Wild.

'I'm not about to do anything foolish, Mother,' Mia assured her. 'And you can set your mind at rest about Bram sweeping me off my feet. He isn't the wild philanderer he's made out to be. Anyway, I'm just an employee, remember?' There was an unconsciously pensive note in her voice that brought a furrow to her mother's brow. She gave Mia an unexpected hug.

'Just...take care, Mia. And if you are determined to see your father, well, I won't try to stop you. But...don't expect too much, will you?'

Mia shook her head, and gave her mother a quick hug in return. Her mother had just given her her blessing—or as close to one as she was likely to get.

That wasn't all that had happened in the days leading up to their departure. Bram went to see his doctor, and when he came back to the car, where Mia was waiting for him, he had had his plaster removed. When he showed her she felt her heart dive to her toes.

'Now you won't need me to go to Italy with you!' The words burst from her.

'Don't be silly, Mia. Of course you're still coming with me. Don't you *want* to come? Don't you *want* to meet your father?'

'Yes, but——'

'Then that's that. Besides, I've already told Nathan you're coming, and he'd never forgive me if I turned up without you. He's delighted you want to see him, and he's very anxious to see *you*. In fact, he tried to see you while he was in Australia last September, but you were overseas at the time with your mother.'

'Oh,' she gulped, not trusting her voice at that moment to say any more. Her father had made an attempt to see her? She'd had no idea. In September she and her mother and brother Paul had been touring New Zealand. He must have found out, and then gone back to Italy without leaving a message. She might never have known now if she hadn't told Bram that Nathan was her father.

Bram tactfully steered the conversation back into a less emotional vein. 'Aren't you pleased that I've got the use of my hand back? I have to have some physio treatment, but by the time we fly out it should be as good as new.'

She nodded and smiled at him—a radiant smile that lit up her delicate face. She *was* pleased for him. But it was relief that had brought the smile—relief that she was still going to Italy with him. It wasn't only the thought of meeting her father...after all, that mightn't even work out yet, however much they both might want the meeting. It wasn't even the thought of visiting Europe for the first time. It was the thought of being close to Bram. What was the point in denying it? So long as she only admitted it to herself!

In those last days before they boarded the plane, busy as they both were, she and Bram seemed to grow closer—even though there were no more passionate kisses between them. It was as if Bram had made a deliberate decision not to risk any kind of emotional confrontation at this time, and she refused to dwell on why. In fact, she was grateful to him because she didn't think she could bear it—she already felt emotional enough at the thought of confronting her father in a few days without having to deal with her feelings for Bram as well. And yet, even so, she could feel the bond between them growing day by day. It would be fuelled by a warm look, the brush of his hand against hers, the mingling of their breath as they pored over a guide book on Italy together, and, incredibly, even when they clashed verbally over an exchange of ideas, or over something that came up at the office. She didn't dare examine too deeply what was happening, for fear it might be like a bubble and burst.

And now at last they were on their way, and she realised that she felt excited, and expectant—even hopeful—whereas before she had felt painfully churned up and apprehensive. Had Bram deliberately gone out of his way to be kind to her this past week, guessing the emotional state she was in—well, guessing part of it, at any rate—and wanting to make things easier for her? Or dared she hope that there was more to this new rapport between them than mere kindness, more than a mere wish on Bram's part to keep her emotions on an even keel until she met up with her father? Was it...could it be possible that he was beginning to genuinely care for her? Had he finally decided to turn his back on Natasha, knowing there was no longer any hope of winning her back?

Her own love for Bram had been growing stronger daily, much as she had tried to fight against it. The thought of leaving him, of never seeing his beloved face again, had become more than she could bear. Was she being a fool, allowing her pride, and the fear of possible heartbreak later, to stifle any hope she might have of a closer relationship with him? Her fingers tightened on the arm of her seat. Sometimes, Mia, you have to go after what you want in life... or the chance just might pass you by.

'Nervous?' Bram asked, reaching for her hand.

She turned to face him, tilting her chin as she said, 'No. Not with you here.'

Despite her new resolution, she tensed, expecting to see some sign of withdrawal, or restraint. But he smiled— that glorious smile of his, that these days, more and more, brought a softening warmth to his eyes. She felt a lump rising in her throat.

'That's my girl.'

She swallowed her relief. 'Do *you* ever feel nervous?' she asked curiously.

He raised her hand to his lips and kissed the tips of her fingers, one by one. 'Not with you here.'

They both laughed, and the bond between them seemed that much closer.

She enjoyed every minute of the long flight to Rome. The first-class menu offered superb meals and equally fine wines, though most of the time she stuck to juices and mineral water, not wanting to emerge too jet lagged from the flight. In quiet moments she pored over an Italian phrase book she had bought during the week, determined to learn at least a smattering of useful Italian words and phrases, and she laughed along with Bram as they watched an award-winning comedy film. As the lights were switched off and silence fell over the aircraft, their comfortable lie-back seats allowed them to have a good sleep on the way. So that when they finally arrived at Rome airport the thought of immediately facing another fifty-minute flight to Florence was not too daunting.

This time it was a small aircraft, which landed early in the afternoon at the domestic airport in Florence, after a scenic flight over the undulating mist-shrouded hills of Tuscany, giving tantalising glimpses of quaint medieval towns, golden fields of maize, and neat rows of vines and olive trees.

They caught a taxi to their hotel in central Florence, arriving—after a hair-raising ride through the city's chaotic traffic—at their five-star hotel, where they were shown to adjoining rooms on the second floor, over-looking the awe-inspiring Duomo, the great cathedral of Florence, close by.

'They say it's best to adjust to local time on arrival,' Bram advised. 'So, if you're not too fatigued, let's take a wander around town before dinner, and then we'll have an early night. I want you well rested for when we visit the Royces tomorrow.'

The Royces...Nathan and Anna...her father and stepmother. Mia drew in a deep, tremulous breath.

But within minutes she had forgotten about tomorrow in the excitement of discovering Florence. The streets and the beautiful squares, or piazzas, were so crowded with people that it was impossible to walk a straight line, and crossing a street in the buzzing, tangled traffic was heart-stoppingly hazardous. But the buildings were beautiful, with an aristocratic elegance that took Mia's breath away. They came to the banks of the Arno River, and strolled across the picturesque Ponte Vecchio, peering into the gold and silver jewellery shops and dodging other tourists as they wove their way among the street sellers who had spread their cheap wares the length of the bridge. Mia bought a scarf from one, a leather belt from another, just for fun, but she shook her head when Bram asked if she'd like to look inside any of the jewellery shops.

'No, thanks—I'd like to just window shop today,' she said with a smile. She had seen the prices. These shops were for rich tourists with money to burn. There must be other shops in Florence for the likes of Mia James.

Bram smiled back at her, with a tenderness in his eyes that set her pulses racing. 'You're right . . . plenty of time later for shopping. Florence abounds with jewellery shops, leather shops, smart boutiques. Best to wait till you're over your jet lag. Ditto the museums and churches and art galleries. Culture requires time . . . and stamina. Neither of which we have today. A bite of dinner and a good sleep are what we need right now. I know of this great little place . . . centuries old. Follow me.'

Halfway across a humming piazza, they paused to admire a beautiful sculpture and fountain. Mia was still looking up as she moved on, thinking her path was clear. Too late she heard the sickening screech of tyres as a car, appearing from nowhere, bore down on her.

She would have been under the car's wheels if Bram's hand hadn't shot out and grabbed her, roughly hauling her back out of its path.

'For heaven's sake, Mia, do you want to get yourself killed?'

She looked shakily up at him, and felt a shuddering reaction when she saw not anger, but *anguish* in his eyes. And he was clasping her shoulders as if he would never let her go.

'Bram...it's all right. I'm fine.' She had never seen him looking so...vulnerable, would never have imagined that he would be vulnerable to anything again, after Natasha. Still less would she have imagined that *she* would ever be the one offering *him* comfort and reassurance.

He pulled her close, holding her fiercely against him, his face buried in her hair. 'Damn it, Mia, I couldn't bear to lose you now!'

Her eyes widened. 'Bram?' There was a trembling enquiry in her voice.

He raised his head and looked down at her, his eyes dark and burning, his pupils enlarged to deep black pools. 'You must know how I feel about you, Mia...by now.'

She felt breathless. 'No. No, I don't. You could try...telling me.'

He pulled her back towards the sculpture, disregarding the other tourists and locals bustling by. 'I was waiting...I wasn't going to say anything yet. I thought you had enough emotional excitement to contend with just now...meeting Nathan tomorrow.'

'I think I can cope with a bit more,' she pressed.

'You're going to make me say it, aren't you? Right here in the middle of the piazza...'

'You seem to be having some difficulty getting it out,' she teased, her chin raised provocatively.

'This isn't my idea of the ideal romantic setting...with car horns and traffic and hordes of people milling around.'

'What could be more romantic than a piazza in Florence...with that tumbling fountain, and those pigeons fluttering around us, and the sound of church bells in the distance...?'

'OK. You win.' Suddenly he was serious, the laughter fading from his eyes. 'Mia, I love you. Dear heaven, *how* I love you! You're everything I've ever wanted in a woman.'

She gulped. Everything? Even in her happiness, an image of Natasha's lovely face swam in front of her.

'Don't you believe me, Mia?'

'Yes... I don't know... I want to, but—Bram, when you heard I had broken up with Richard, you made it plain that *you* would never want me.'

'Is that what you thought?' He pushed a stray tendril of hair away from her cheek. 'I wanted to give you some breathing-space, Mia... I didn't want you turning to me *on the rebound*. I wanted to be sure that you knew what you were doing, that whatever you felt for me—if you did feel anything—was going to match what I felt for you.'

'Oh, Bram... I don't know what to say.'

'You could put me out of my misery and tell me that you love me and never want to leave me.'

At each word he uttered she could feel her qualms, her doubts, dissolving. Joy flowed through her. Bram loved her, and he was anxious to hear that she loved him!

'I love you, Bram...and I never want to leave you.'
She lifted her face to his, and, oblivious of the curious,
watchful eyes around them, Bram bent his head and
pressed his lips to hers, sealing their love with a kiss.
Happiness flowed through her. It all seemed too good
to be true...

When their chauffeur-driven car arrived to pick them up
the next morning, Mia felt as if she was drifting along
in a dream. She was no longer apprehensive about
meeting her father. Why should she be, when Nathan
was as anxious as she to mend the rift between them?

The previous evening had been the most wonderful
evening of her life. To begin with, dinner at the cen-
turies-old Il Bargello *ristorante*, with mouthwatering
cannelloni and salad, fine white wine from the Orvieto
district, delicious ice-cream, and the friendliest service
in the world...and, above all, Bram facing her across
the table, with love in his eyes.

'It's a pity we don't have more time this trip,' he had
said to her. 'There's so much I want you to see.
Michelangelo's *David* at the Academy, the fabulous
paintings at the Uffizi, the glorious sculptures at the
Bargello Museum, the leather shops, the jewellery. We'll
have a couple of spare days while we're here, but it won't
be enough. We'll have to come back to Italy for our
honeymoon.'

Her breath caught in her lungs. 'Is that a proposal?'

'You look surprised.'

'I thought you were anti-marriage.'

'You've restored my faith in women...in love...in
marriage...in the whole bit.'

'Oh, Bram.'

'Is that a yes?'

'Yes!' She didn't even need time to think. 'My mother will be bowled over,' she confessed. 'She warned me not to fall for you. She said marriage was not on your agenda.'

'That shows how mistaken a mother can be. When she hears that my intentions are honourable do you think I'll be able to win her over?'

She smiled, shaking her head at him. 'I'm sure you will.'

And then afterwards... Mia's eyes misted over with emotion at the memory of it. Jet lagged as she was, and despite knowing that Bram was anxious for her to have a good night's rest and would have been content with the lingering kiss he gave her at her door, she had, only minutes later, knocked on the adjoining door between their rooms, and come to *him*, dressed only in the flimsy nightgown she had once worn so coyly in his presence.

'I know you don't ravish virgins,' she had said shyly, her soft voice trembling slightly, with emotion, not fear, 'but what if a virgin were to... ravish *you*?'

Bram, already stripped to his underpants, stood immobile for such a long moment that she nearly lost her courage and ran. Until she saw the deep longing in his eyes.

A knot rose in her throat. 'You said once that you hoped I would come to you,' she said. 'Well... I've come.'

She stepped towards him as she spoke, her bare arms outstretched, her eyes softly inviting. Wonderingly, he caught her hands in his, holding her for a moment at arm's length.

'Are you sure, Mia?' he asked huskily.

She nodded. 'You're not too tired?' she asked provocatively.

'You...devil,' he growled, his fingers slipping along her arms. 'You irresistible little devil.'

He crushed her to him, his mouth hungrily covering hers, sending the pit of her stomach into a wild swirl. She clung to him, her fingers digging into his back, exulting in the feel of his smooth naked skin under her hands as their bodies strained against each other in a fierce, passionate explosion that seemed to go on forever.

At last he dragged his lips away, groaning, 'Mia! You're like a wild flame! You're inflaming *me*!' and trailed a burning path down the vulnerable, pulsing cord at the edge of her neck, burying his mouth in the gentle hollow. His touch was an exquisite torture as he caressed each delicate indentation along the base of her throat before seeking the lobe of her ear, taking it between his teeth and biting the sensitive flesh with just enough pressure to send a tremor raking through her body.

'Is the fire burning you too, Mia?' he whispered against her ear, and she groaned in assent. He drew his head back and held her away from him, sliding the straps of her gown down over her shoulders, easing the thin slither of silk from her breasts until it slipped down into a small heap on the carpet at her feet.

His eyes were dark and languorous as they took in her slim curves, and she felt her breasts grow heavy beneath his gaze, their rosy peaks burgeoning in anticipation of the sweet torture that only he could provide.

'You're beautiful, Mia,' he said hoarsely, his fingers tracing a path down the column of her throat to the swollen peak of her breast, caressing it gently with his thumb before sliding to cup its fullness in his hand.

She slid her arms round his waist and pressed him against her, whimpering in a mixture of arousal and tension at the intimate contact of flesh on flesh.

She felt his body shudder under her touch. 'Mia...mine! If you only knew the effect you have on me! I'm putty in your arms!'

His voice trembled slightly, and her eyes widened with incredulity, for the second time that day, that this man who had always seemed so tough and invincible, this man who commanded such a huge empire, could be reduced to any degree of vulnerability.

'Oh, Bram,' she whispered, her eyes prickling.

'I'm all yours,' he said huskily. 'Now and forever.'

Her heartbeat quickened as warmth flooded through her veins, filling her body with a delicious glow. 'I love you, Bram!' She raised her hands to capture his face, pulling it down to hers as she initiated a kiss that left him in no doubt of her feelings. Her heart was in her eyes, in the touch of her lips as it roamed the harsh contours of his face, in the heat of her body as she arched against him.

With a soft moan, he lifted her off her feet and laid her on the bed, sliding down beside her, kissing and caressing her in ways that sensitised every inch of her flesh, twisting her nerves into exquisite expectancy of more and more sensation.

As his thumbs stroked her taut nipples she smothered the cry of need that rose in her throat by pressing her mouth into his shoulder. It was only when he shuddered against her that she realised that she had bitten him. Her body flushed with shame until she heard him groan, 'Oh, Mia, you want me as much as I want you, don't you? Don't you?' he demanded thickly, rolling her over so that she was lying on her back and he was looking down into the vulnerable oval of her face.

'Yes, Bram, yes!' But she didn't need to say anything. Her face and body gave her away.

She heard him mutter something, but his words were lost against her skin as his mouth plundered the tender curve of her throat, sucking and biting into her soft skin until she was shivering with a pleasure that reached right down to her toes. Her inexperience, her lack of sexual expertise, were forgotten as she responded blindly to the inflammatory combination of his touch and his desire. Wherever his hand and mouth touched her, her skin burned, her body melting with heat and pleasure.

'Bram!' she gasped, giving herself up to the voluptuous heat flooding through her body, opening her lips to the demanding thrust of his tongue as it mirrored the fierce movement of his hips against her body. She felt a savage clawing need to be closer and closer to him, to want to absorb him completely within her.

'I want to taste every delectable inch of you . . . like this,' he moaned against her mouth, his teeth taking tiny bites at the swollen fullness of her lips, while his caressing hands were like fire on her body. 'And I'm going to teach you to want to do the same to me.'

He didn't need to teach her—she was already aching to do so. Bram seemed to have released a deep vein of erotic sensuality in her that no man, not even Richard, had ever come near to touching.

His lips traced the line of her collarbone, and moved down over her body, feathering between her breasts and then moving with tantalising slowness over their swollen curves.

She cried out at the sensations caused by the fierce sucking movement of his mouth against her sensitive nipple, but when he stopped she ached for him to continue the erotic caress.

Already, shamelessly, her body was melting in anticipation of more intimate caresses; already she was longing to caress him with the same intimacy, eager to learn everything about him that he wanted to teach her, overwhelmed by the flood of love and desire that poured through her, obliterating all restraints.

Her hands stroked tremulously over his skin, registering with wonder his reaction to her touch. Passionately, she touched her mouth to the hard flatness of his stomach.

'Mia, for heaven's sake! I can't stand any more!'

He rolled away from her. 'Are you sure, Mia, that this is what you want?' She saw anguish mingled with the longing in his eyes.

'Oh, Bram, yes. Yes!'

'I want all of you, Mia,' he said huskily.

'I want you too, Bram,' she said, knowing it was right, knowing this was the time, the place, and the man she could truly give herself to.

When he finally moved to take her she welcomed him with an ecstatic sigh, and found herself spinning into a whirlpool of sensual delight, his name bursting from her lips on a long, moaning note as wave after wave of intense sensation broke through her body, building to a crest of almost anguished expectancy. She heard herself cry out, and in the next instant felt the explosive release of his body mingling its warmth with hers, sending ripples of intense pleasure radiating through her entire being.

Afterwards, as they lay trembling in each other's arms, he muttered fiercely, 'I couldn't bear to lose you, Mia. You've given me back the love and trust I never thought I'd find again,' and she stroked his back in blissful wonderment and whispered,

'I'll always love you, Bram. Always.'

*   *   *

Mia wondered if the Tuscan countryside always looked as beautiful as this in the spring, or if she was seeing it through rose-tinted spectacles. No wonder her father had wanted to stay here forever... the beauty of the country-side must have inspired many a painting in the years he had been living here.

They were meeting Nathan at his home, leaving the mill and the signing of the documents until tomorrow. Private matters first, Bram had decreed, business second, and she appreciated his thoughtfulness, even as she felt herself trembling at the thought of visiting her father's home. Would his wife Anna resent his long-lost daughter coming into their lives?

She needn't have worried. Both Nathan and Anna met them at the door of their quaint stone villa deep in Tuscany's beautiful Chianti district, and both were smiling with a warmth she never would have expected. Mia felt a wave of emotion at the sight of her father. She could see that they shared a resemblance, though his hair had faded to a sandy colour and, whereas she was petite, he was tall and lanky. But his eyes were the same grey-green as her own and there was a sensitivity about his features that was reminiscent of her own deli-cate bone-structure. And he had a most irrepressible smile. She could see how easy it must have been for her mother, at the tender age of eighteen, to have been swept off her feet by him.

She saw tears mist his eyes, and blinked away a sus-picious prickle in her own. He held out his arms to her, and next moment they were hugging each other, and the lost years seemed to melt away, along with the bitterness and the doubts that she had lived with for so long.

'I couldn't believe it when Bram said my daughter worked for him.' Nathan's voice trembled slightly, his accent still noticeably Australian after all these years. 'My dear, I'd given up hope of ever seeing you again.'

'Bram told me you tried to contact me when you were in Australia last year,' Mia said shyly. 'I'm sorry I was away at the time. My mother and I were touring New Zealand in September.'

'Nat, why don't you take Mia for a stroll round the garden?' Anna suggested. 'Bram and I will have a chat while I prepare our lunch.' Her voice was deep and warm, and her excellent English was softly accented. She was not a classic beauty—her nose and her mouth were too large for that—but her intelligent dark eyes and her warm smile gave her a special beauty of her own. Her hair was streaked with grey and tied in a thick braid that reached almost to her waist.

Nathan tucked Mia's arm in his and led her outside, where they strolled through his terraced garden, shaded by a row of parasol pines.

'I've often wondered about you, Mia,' Nathan confessed, pressing her hand. 'You've grown from a beautiful baby into a lovely woman. I'm sorry I missed seeing you grow up.'

'You could have—if you'd stayed at home with us,' Mia returned, with more sorrow in her tone than bitterness.

'My dear...' Nathan stopped walking, and swung her round to face him '...your mother and I...our marriage was already over before I left Australia. We had realised by then that it was never going to work out. My art meant everything to me, and your mother couldn't understand that. She wanted me to give it up and settle down to a regular nine-to-five job. I was making very little money... I know it wasn't easy for her. Having to live with her parents put an added strain on our mar-

riage. You were the only thing that kept us together, Mia.
In fact, you were the reason we got married in the first
place.'

'Yes, I always knew it was a shotgun wedding,' Mia
said stolidly.

'No one held a gun to my head, Mia,' Nathan assured
her. 'There was some pressure, admittedly, from your
grandparents, but I did it for your mother, not for them.
We were both very young and imagined we loved each
other enough to make it work. But after two years we
were both older and wiser, and knew we'd been fooling
ourselves. Your mother hated the art world...and I
couldn't give it up. When I was offered the chance to
study art in Italy I had to take it—and that's when our
marriage finally fell apart. Your mother refused to come
with me——'

'Do you blame her?' Mia came gently to her mother's
defence. 'A woman like my mother needs
security...roots. She would never have been able to face
living in a foreign country, with a baby and hardly any
money, not knowing a soul or a word of the language...'

'No, I never blamed her. I suppose it was selfish of
me to go off the way I did. But I was young and
ambitious and impatient, and I simply couldn't turn my
back on the chance of a lifetime. I knew that, whether
I went or stayed, our marriage was over. So why let it
drag on? I believe we did the right thing, parting when
we did. You mother was lucky enough to find a more
suitable partner very quickly...and I was equally blessed
in finding Anna.'

'And I ceased to exist for you,' Mia said with a poign-
ancy she couldn't hide.

'No...never!' Nathan's eyes flashed a denial. 'When
your mother wrote and asked me for a divorce so that

she could marry Martin James she begged me to stop writing to you . . . and not to send any cards or presents in the future. She said it would only confuse you.'

Mia stared at him. 'You . . . wrote to me?'

'For a while I did. You were barely three years old when I stopped writing—you would have been too young to remember.'

'But later . . . Mother could have given them to me later!'

'Mia . . . she wanted you to forget me. I can understand that. I had walked out on you. I had abandoned you. I had lost my right to you. In her eyes I had put my ambition before my family. And it's true—I had. My art came first. Don't blame your mother, Mia. Blame me.'

Mia shook her head angrily. 'How could she do that to me? She let me think you didn't care about me . . .'

'Mia, you must see it from her side. She wanted to protect you—to give you a stable family life, without the pain and confusion of being torn two ways. It wasn't as if I lived close enough to come and visit you. Martin wanted to adopt you as his own daughter, and she wanted you to look on him as your father. She wanted you to be secure and happy, Mia. And so did I. I had found happiness by then with Anna . . . the least I could do was to give you and your mother the same chance. Perhaps what we did was wrong, but——' he shrugged '—we were both thinking of you.'

Mia swallowed her anger. In their own way they had both meant well. Both had wanted to get on with their own separate lives, with the minimum of pain and confusion. And Martin *had* been like a father to her. She had never lacked love. And neither, she knew, had

Nathan. 'You love Anna very much, don't you?' she said.

'With all my heart and body and soul. We are soul mates, Mia ... we share everything. Your mother and I had nothing in common—except you. I can't tell you how happy I am that you have come to me at last. I always hoped you would, one day.'

'Oh, Nathan...' The name came naturally, solving her earlier dilemma about what to call him. 'If only I had known how you felt. I would have contacted you earlier ... somehow ...'

'I was tempted many a time to write to you,' Nathan admitted. 'But I didn't want to intrude on your life ... I felt I had lost the right. It was only when I came back to Australia last year, for the first time, that I was able to pluck up the courage to call you. When there was no answer I made some enquiries, and discovered that you and your mother and stepbrother were all overseas. It seemed as if fate was determined to keep us apart.'

'Until now,' Mia said, smiling at him. 'Nathan...Bram says you and Anna have three children. Are they at home today?' It was amazing how easy it was to ask. A week ago, a day ago, she wouldn't have found it so easy!

'Sadly, no, they're all away at school or university. I will show you their photographs when we go back to the house. But first, my dear ... I want to hear everything you have been doing for the past twenty years.'

CHAPTER TEN

MIA and Nathan were all smiles when they joined the others for lunch on the balustraded terrace overlooking the distant vine-clad hills. Only Nathan's children were missing from what was turning out to be a heart-warming family get-together. Mia no longer had any qualms about meeting her half-brothers and half-sister, and hoped that the chance would arise before too long. *Perhaps on our honeymoon,* she thought dreamily, hugging the memory of Bram's promise in her heart.

Nathan hadn't asked any personal questions about her relationship with Bram during the time they were alone together—they barely had time to catch up on their lost years before Anna called them to lunch. And Mia wasn't surprised when Bram said nothing either. He would look on this as her day...hers and Nathan's. He wouldn't want anything else to intrude. Not today. Time enough tomorrow to tell Nathan and Anna the news when Bram and Nathan met up again to sign the partnership papers.

During the afternoon Nathan and Anna, anxious for Mia to see something of the Tuscan countryside around their home, drove them to the scenic sixteenth-century town of Vinci, birthplace of Leonardo da Vinci. An old stone castle had been converted into the Vinci Museum, where working models had been made of Leonardo's numerous inventions, using his detailed sketches and instructions. They spent some time browsing happily among the models, admiring the genius of the man who had invented everything from bicycles to scuba-diving equipment, from steam engines to hang-gliding appar-

atus, from traction engines to aeroplanes. Through the
windows of the museum Mia caught enticing glimpses
of the rolling Tuscan hills, where quaint houses with
terracotta rooftops nestled among the vines and the olive
groves, with cypress trees and pencil pines providing
splashes of deeper colour, and she could understand how
Nathan had fallen in love with the place and why he had
never wanted to leave.

They had a delicious pasta and *vino* meal on their way
back to Nathan's villa, where their driver Lorenzo had
arranged to meet them. While they were waiting for
Lorenzo to arrive, Nathan and Anna showed Bram and
Mia some of their paintings. Anna's special talent lay in
soft watercolour landscapes, Nathan's in robust oils,
pulsing with colour and intense rhythms. He presented
her with one of them, titled *Tuscan Harvest*, a riot of
earthy greens and golds beneath a whirling blue sky.

All in all, a wonderful day. Though Bram kept largely
in the background, there were stolen glances and shared
smiles to remind Mia of the delicious secret they shared.
Several times she noticed Nathan watching them. And
she would have sworn, once or twice, that she saw a
flicker of concern in his eyes. It was puzzling... the only
faint blot on an otherwise perfect day, and it niggled at
her until it was time to go.

'Give me a last minute alone with my daughter,'
Nathan pleaded when Lorenzo arrived to pick them up.

'I'll walk Bram to the car,' Anna said, and as she and
Bram turned to go Bram brushed Mia's shoulder with
the tips of his fingers, and they exchanged a brief smile,
Mia following him with her eyes as he strolled off with
Anna.

She felt Nathan's arm slide round her waist. 'You love
him, don't you, Mia?'

She turned, startled. 'Is it that obvious?'

'It is to anyone with eyes. And he loves you too.'

'Yes!' Her eyes shone with a confidence she wouldn't have dreamt of twenty-four hours ago.

'But... will you be content with an affair, Mia?'

So that was what had been niggling at him! She felt relief dance through her. 'Bram has asked me to marry him,' she confided, smiling. 'It... only happened last night. It's not official yet.'

Her smile faltered when she saw not joy, but consternation in Nathan's sun-crinkled eyes.

'I never thought he'd marry.' Nathan's brow furrowed. 'Mia, how well do you know Bram?'

Mia took a deep breath. 'I know about Natasha, if that's what you mean.'

'You know why she walked out on him?' Nathan was watching her closely, his eyes perturbed.

'She left him to marry someone else—a friend of the family with loads of money and a socially impeccable background,' she said lightly.

'That's what Bram has let you think?' Nathan seemed to hesitate, and then, with a sigh, he said, 'Well, he would hardly tell you the truth, I suppose; that she left him because he was...unfaithful. Only three days before their wedding-day. Can you wonder that she ran out on him?'

The blood drained from Mia's face. 'I don't believe it!' she whispered. 'He *loved* Natasha! He wouldn't have done that to her.'

Nathan's eyes softened in sympathy. 'He's a passionate, hot-blooded man, Mia. Even from this distance, I know that he has a certain... reputation for not sticking to one woman. I gather he has appetites that a single woman would find difficult to satisfy. Why do you think he has never married in all these years?' he asked gently. 'That sounds to me like a man who feels he can't trust himself to remain faithful to one woman!'

Mia felt a cold hand close over her heart. She had always known that Bram was a virile, passionate man, powerfully attractive to women. But for him to... No, it couldn't be true! He wouldn't... And yet at the same time a memory nagged at her and she bit back a moan, recalling what Russ Masters had said about that terrible time, hinting at rumours he had refused to repeat. Naturally, as Bram's close friend and most trusted business colleague, he would have closed his ears to such rumours, or tried to. But how did they start in the first place? Oh, dear lord! she thought.

Nathan took her hand and gave it a quick squeeze. 'Look, maybe he has changed...a man *can* change, Mia. But... tread carefully, my dear, won't you? Take time to get to know him better before you commit yourself to anything permanent. Having discovered you again after all these years, I find you're rather precious to me. I wouldn't want to see you get hurt. Or... suffering in an unhappy marriage.' It was obvious that it pained him to talk about Bram this way. He was about to become Bram's partner, after all. And that made it all ring horribly true.

'Mia, just...don't rush into anything,' Nathan begged. 'Promise me that?'

She nodded, blinking away a prickle of hot tears. She felt as if a desolate black void had opened in front of her, where only minutes ago there had been nothing but blissful dreams.

'Mia, what's wrong?' Bram demanded when she froze at the brush of his lips on her nape as she rummaged in her bag for her door key, Lorenzo having moments earlier dropped them off at their hotel. 'You've been quiet ever since we left Nathan's. I know you must have a lot to think about—it's been quite a day for you, meeting your father after all these years—but...it's more than that, isn't it?' There was a roughness in his voice, and she knew that her withdrawal a moment ago was responsible for it.

She fumbled as she tried to push the key into the door. 'I'm just tired,' she said, her voice cracking as she spoke. She needed time to think, to decide what to do.

His hand closed over hers, turning the key so that he could open the door. 'Mia, don't lie to me,' he growled, almost pushing her inside. 'If there's something bothering you I want to hear it. Now!'

'Don't *push* me!' she burst out, wheeling round to face him, her eyes wide and stark in her pale face. His touch had sparked a blaze of heat through her veins, and anger seemed the best way to deal with it.

'For heaven's sake, Mia, what's got into you?' He gripped her shoulders and gave her an impatient shake, and she gasped as she struggled to free herself, knowing that if she stayed in his arms she would weaken.

'Let me go! You're hurting me!'

His hands only tightened their grip, and, feeling their iron strength, she gave a muffled sob and went limp in his grasp. 'Please,' she whispered. 'Let me go! L-leave me alone. I—I want to go to bed!'

He released her with a muttered oath, standing over her, his eyes glowing with a savage inner fire. 'So...now you've got what you wanted...to meet your father...I've outlived my usefulness—is that it?'

Her eyes flew wide. 'No!' she choked. 'No, it's not that!'

'Then what the hell is it?'

She could see that he wasn't going to leave until they'd had it out. 'I—it's *you*, Bram!' she gasped, tears welling in her eyes. 'I—I can't marry a man who... I—I just can't!' She twisted away from him and burst into tears.

He stood still, shock holding him immobile. She saw his lips thin with anger, and then his voice lashed her like a whip. 'So...it's going to be history repeating itself, is it? You're going to run out on me...just like she did! What is it, Mia?' he taunted, contempt hardening his eyes. 'Last night too much of a shock to you? Having second thoughts about marrying a real flesh and blood man? I suppose you want to go crawling back to that undemanding wimp you were engaged to? You women make me sick! You're all tarred with the same brush!'

She paled. 'You don't think much of women...do you, Bram?' she whispered, misery sweeping over her.

'What is that supposed to mean?'

She raised a hand to dash away her tears. 'You m-must have hurt a lot of women in your time. You even hurt the woman you were planning to marry. Natasha, the girl who would have married *you*, if you hadn't——'

She broke off with a strangled gasp as he caught her wrist in a steel-like grasp. 'If I hadn't—what, Mia?'

She could have bitten her tongue out. Why, oh, why hadn't she kept her mouth shut—at least until she had had time to think things over, or, perhaps more important, until after Bram and Nathan had signed their contract? If Bram refused to sign now, she would be responsible!

Into the deathly silence, Bram's voice, steel-edged and ruthless, stabbed the air. 'Finish it, Mia! If I hadn't...what?'

She heaved a shuddering sigh. 'If you hadn't gone to bed with another woman only three days before your wedding-day!'

She flinched at the blaze of fury in his eyes. 'Where the hell did you hear that load of codswallop?'

She bit her lip, not wanting to bring Nathan into it. She heard herself floundering. 'People talk, Bram... To do a thing like that, three days before your wedding... *Are you denying it?*' Hope flared in her eyes. If he denied it, could she believe him? Heaven knew, she wanted to!

His own eyes were as hard as flint...and as she watched they narrowed to dangerous slits. 'You were fine until you had that moment alone with Nathan this evening... *He's* the one who's filled your head with this garbage. Hell! The man I'm considering going into partnership with, going around spreading a charming little gem like that!'

'Bram, no, he hasn't been...he wouldn't...it's not like that!' she protested, squeezing her hands to her heaving chest. 'He only told me because he... Bram, he guessed there was something between us, and when he knew you had asked me to marry you it was only then that he... Bram, he's my father! He—he was concerned about me.'

'Well, then, we mustn't give him anything to be concerned about...must we?' She flinched at the icy contempt in Bram's voice. 'I'll say goodnight, Mia...and sweet dreams.' He barely glanced at her as he swung away. 'I suggest you have breakfast in your room in the morning. Be ready to leave at nine. You and I have an appointment to keep!'

'Bram, don't go!' she gasped, but he was already gone, the bang of the slamming door echoing behind him. What did he mean—appointment? To sign the partnership papers, did he mean? But that wasn't scheduled until later in the morning—and, anyway, it didn't involve her. A new fear clutched her heart. Did he mean an appointment at the airport in Florence? Was he taking her home...without signing the papers? And, once he had her home, would that be the last she ever saw of him?

She threw herself down on the bed and let the tears flow anew, thrashing about on her pillow in despair and confusion, still not sure if Bram's anger was the fury of a man caught out...or if his reaction was that of a desperately wronged man. And, if that proved to be so, would Bram ever forgive her for believing such a rumour?

Right on nine o'clock, a sharp rap on her door brought her running to open it. 'Lorenzo's waiting.' Bram's voice sounded as hard, as implacable as it had the night before. His brow was lowered, his expression closed and cold. He might have been a stranger.

'Bram...' Her hand fluttered out, but he was already turning, striding away from her. 'Bram, where are we going?' she called after him. He hadn't said anything about her luggage, which she had packed, just in case.

'You'll find out soon enough.'

If they were checking out he would have told her. She snatched up her handbag and stumbled after him. He was deliberately doing this to make her sweat, to punish her! Well, maybe she deserved it—if what Nathan had told her was untrue, as Bram's reaction seemed to indicate. Either way, she could have lost Bram forever, through her own clumsiness, her lack of trust...

Bram made her sit in the back seat by herself, while he sat in the front next to Lorenzo. They followed the same route as yesterday, and she soon realised that they were heading for Nathan's villa. So Bram planned a confrontation! Her heart skipped a beat, and then settled into a thumping, ominous tattoo. Would any of them still be speaking to each other at the end of it? Would Bram speak to her ever again?

Nathan met them at the door. He looked anxious, but defiant, and gave Mia's arm an encouraging squeeze. Anna was keeping discreetly out of sight.

'We can talk in here,' Nathan said, leading the way into a rather cluttered den, lined with bookshelves. 'Would you like to sit here?' he invited, waving Mia into a chair. Bram chose to remain standing, as did Nathan.

'It's time we cleared the air about one or two things,' Bram said grimly. Not being a man to beat about the bush, he fixed Nathan with a piercing stare and demanded curtly, 'Where did you hear this cock-and-bull story about me being unfaithful to Natasha?'

Nathan cleared his throat. 'Whatever the truth is, Bram, I want you to know that I've never repeated what I heard to another soul... until yesterday. I never would have brought it up then if it hadn't been my own daughter who was involved...'

'Who?' Bram barked. 'Who told you?'

Nathan shrugged. 'I had a visit from Kevin Dysan around the time we were looking for a partner——'

'Hell!' Bram threw up his hands. 'Kevin Dysan! And you believed him? He's one of my bitterest rivals, for heaven's sake!'

Nathan thrust out his bottom lip. 'I admit that, at the time he told me, I did wonder if he might have been trying to discredit you. But he swore it came directly from Natasha's mother... He's a friend of the family...'

Bram swore. 'Natasha's mother! Well, that figures. She never could stand me. I was too rough, too wild, too much of an unknown entity for her taste. Mm, it does make sense,' he brooded aloud. 'She wouldn't have relished those rumours about her daughter leaving me for a man with more money. Casting me as the villain would have suited her far better.'

Nathan was still frowning. 'But, if Natasha knew her mother was spreading an evil rumour like that, why didn't she deny it?'

Bram smiled grimly. 'Natasha has never had much...backbone. And going public about the real reason she left me would have been...difficult for her, I grant her that. Because it wasn't Kennedy-Ford's money she left me for. She admitted as much the other night. It seems,' he said drily, 'she found me too...potent for her taste.'

'What do you mean?' Mia forced the words out.

'Oh, don't worry,' Bram said, his eyes hardening. 'I didn't force myself on her or anything like that. And I certainly didn't play around with other women—I believe in one woman at a time. But hell—I did get damned frustrated at times. She was so...passive, unresponsive. I felt like shaking some feeling into her. The closer our wedding-day came, the more she seemed to be withdrawing from me. I thought she was worried about our wedding night—she was a gentle little thing...innocent, a virgin. I tried to be gentle with her, but I'm not a naturally gentle person. I have strong feelings...I'm passionate, tempestuous—that's just me. I was baffled by the change in her—she was changing in front of my eyes from a warm, affectionate girl into a cold, unresponsive creature I barely knew. In frustration one night I lost my temper. I shouted at her, demanding to know if she felt anything at all for me. I just wanted her to show a bit of *feeling*. She broke away and ran from the room in tears. That was the last time I saw her.'

A throbbing silence fell. The air was static, yet vibrant with feeling, and Mia smothered an impulse to leap up and throw her arms around him, to let him feel, without the need for words, the sympathy flowing from her. Then abruptly the silence was cut by a harsh laugh from Bram.

'She ran off the next day with Kennedy-Ford, leaving me a note saying she had made a terrible mistake—that I couldn't give her what she wanted, and he, her old pal Tim, could. What was I to think? I assumed that she meant money, background, all the things that Kennedy-Ford was offering. It was only later, years later, after I had built up my business and restored my house, driven by some demon to achieve more and more, to prove to all and sundry, I guess, that I was a force to be reckoned with... it was only when I had thrown off that demon that I began to wonder if it could be me, the *man*—a red-blooded man with strong passions—that she had run away from, and nothing to do with money, position, and background.'

He ran a distracted hand through his crop of silver-streaked hair. 'I had a chance to find out last week when we met again at that dinner dance—and, being a little older and braver now, she admitted it was true. She hadn't left me for Kennedy-Ford's money or anything of that sort—she had left me because I was too over-powering, too demanding, too passionate, as she put it. She had been infatuated, she said—swept off her feet—but, as our wedding-day came closer, reality hit her and she knew she couldn't go through with it. She turned to her faithful pal, Kennedy-Ford, who persuaded her to run off and marry him instead. He, being gentle and undemanding and patient—all the things that I wasn't—was, she had realised in the nick of time, the right man for her after all. But she wasn't brave enough at the time to tell me to my face, hence that cryptic note she left me. It was some time,' he muttered wryly, 'before I realised she had done me a favour by running out on me. It would have been a disaster—she saw that before I did.'

He held up a hand as Mia opened her mouth to speak. He still had more to say. 'I was aware there were rumours going around, but I thought—to hell with them. Let people believe what they like. But I do care about what *you* think, Mia. Last night I reacted angrily because I was hurt that you would give the rumours any credence... but, since nobody has ever denied them, and I know I haven't exactly lived the life of a monk in the years since Natasha ran out on me, how could I expect...?' He broke off impatiently, and said tightly, a pulse throbbing at his temple, 'I brought you here to set the record straight, once and for all. You know it all now. If you choose not to believe it I won't hold it against you.' He stood a moment looking down at Mia, his eyes half closed, hooded. 'I'll leave you with Nathan. You'll want to digest it all, no doubt. No hard feelings, Mia,' he said, making it sound like a farewell, a *goodbye*. 'When you're ready to sign the papers, Nathan, I'll sign.'

'Bram, don't go!' Mia leapt out of her chair and ran to him, seizing his arm. 'Don't you *dare* go away before you've heard what I have to say!'

He stopped, and she saw his expression change, his eyes kindling with something she couldn't define, a look too complex to read. But it gave her the courage to go on.

'I don't *need* to digest anything, Bram—I believe you and I... I'll never forgive myself for doubting you,' she said with a slight tremor in her voice. 'I don't care about the other women you've had since Natasha left you. I only care about *you*, Bram, and being the only woman in your life from now on!' Then, lifting her chin, she said, with a sparkle in her eye, 'But don't you go getting the idea that I think you're perfect, Bram Wild, because you're not! You have a terrible temper... you love to throw your weight around... you love to act the ogre...and you did break your hand punching some poor fellow on the jaw. But *I* don't intend to run away from you, Bram Wild. I *love* you. Even though I was thrown for six by that story about you being unfaithful to Natasha three days before your wedding-day I never stopped loving you, Bram. I never will!'

There was a scuffle, a movement behind them. 'I'll be in the next room with Anna. You two sort it out,' said Nathan, and made his escape. He was shaking his head and trying to stifle a grin, Mia noted foggily.

Bram looked down at her, his lip quirking. 'About my broken hand...' he said. He had moved a step closer— a mere breath away. The small space between them seemed to crackle with leaping electric currents.

'Oh, yes? You're going to tell me at last what really happened?' Mia's eyes were faintly teasing. But her voice was breathless, not quite steady.

'Well, since we're setting the record straight...' Bram was determined to clear the air, once and for all. 'This weed of a journalist was pestering me. He wanted to do a personal profile on me for his newspaper. When I said no he turned nasty. He started taunting me about being jilted at the altar. How did I feel when my fiancée tossed me over three days before our wedding-day to marry a fresh-cheeked young millionaire? When I tried to push past him he grabbed my arm. Was it true that my fiancée had caught me in bed with another woman? Was that the real reason she had left me?'

'Oh, Bram.' Mia's hand fluttered up to touch his arm. She was beginning to understand why he shunned the media.

'I told him to let go of me or I'd have him up for assault.' Bram's jaw tightened. 'But the guy wasn't listening. He tightened his grubby grip on me and said,

''Is it true that you are the father of Natasha Kennedy-Ford's first-born child?'''

As Mia caught her breath, Bram growled, 'That's when I let fly with my fist. The pathetic little creep saw it coming and cowered back against the wall. I should have let him have it. But in the last split-second I let my fist fly past his nose, missing him by a whisker. It was too late to pull back, and I hit the brick wall instead. The side of my fist caught the full impact.' Bram's lip curled. 'The little weasel didn't wait around to offer sympathy—he scuttled off like the miserable creature he was.'

Mia felt a giggle rising in her throat. 'I don't know whether to laugh or cry,' she confessed.

'You could show some sympathy,' Bram said with mock severity.

She reached for his hand and kissed it. 'You're lucky you didn't do more damage.'

'*He's* lucky I didn't damage *him*,' Bram said flatly. His hand closed around hers and he pulled her against him. 'Natasha,' he assured her, sobering, 'was a virgin when she married Kennedy-Ford. Their first child was born prematurely, eight months after they were married. Hence the rumour,' he said ruefully. 'At least the principle parties have always known the truth. And that's all that counts. And now you know too. You know it all. I don't care what anyone else believes, but I want you, Mia, to know the truth. I don't play around. There will never be another woman for me, Mia, as long as I have you.'

She felt her eyes mist over, then begin to ache with unshed tears as he lifted a hand and tenderly traced the outline of her mouth. Bram was a proud man—a strong, self-sufficient man—and she sensed that this was the first time he had ever unburdened himself to anyone, the first time he had ever felt impelled to set the record straight. She felt a rush of love for him, knowing how difficult it must have been for such a man.

'Bram...' curiosity drove her to ask '...what made you choose me to come and work for you in the first place?' She forced out another question. 'Was it because I reminded you of Natasha?'

He touched his hand to her cheek. 'I chose you *despite* the fact that you reminded me of Natasha. It occurred to me that I'd spent years avoiding a certain type of woman—the type of woman I had vowed I would never fall for again. It was stupid. What was I afraid of? That I might be attracted to you, simply because you looked a bit like Natasha—because you were young and fresh-faced and natural, with a similar soft voice?'

As Mia held her breath he shook his head. 'Maybe I wanted to prove to myself that I was immune. Who knows? When I realised that, despite everything, I *was* being drawn to you, I fought it, thinking you would turn out to be like Natasha. I deliberately tried to frighten you off—but you didn't react the way I expected. I came to realise you're nothing like Natasha...you're *you*, Mia...you're unique, special—the embodiment of everything I've been searching for all my life. You're tough, yet gentle. You're open-minded and unspoilt, not jaded or artificial. People and values are more important to you than money or notoriety. You're warm, passionate, brave...you're game to try anything—but not wildly, irresponsibly. And you have a sense of fun, a sense of humour. I love you, Mia, because you're *you*.' A smile touched his lips. 'And, above all, you know how to keep me in line.'

'That's debatable,' said Mia, but she had a lump in her throat as she said it. Now she understood what Bram had meant that time when he had agreed with her that she wasn't Natasha. She had been hurt at the time, thinking that he had meant that no woman could be to him what Natasha had been. But now she knew better. He had never wanted her to be like Natasha. If only she had known that earlier!

Her lips parted and she let out a soft moan as Bram buried his face in her hair and nibbled at her ear, murmuring, 'You're a witch, my darling Mia... You've bewitched *me*. From the moment you first walked into my office I didn't stand a chance.'

'Neither did I...' Mia felt a delicious weakness seeping through her limbs as he dragged his lips across her cheek and captured her mouth, kissing her slowly, thoroughly, in a way that demonstrated very effectively that there were no longer any misunderstandings between them.

In that moment she forgot where she was, even forgot about Nathan waiting anxiously in another room with Anna, until Bram drew back and said, in a low husky voice that simmered with barely checked passion, 'Let's go and find Nathan. After we've signed those partnership papers there's another more personal partnership I'd like to concentrate on.'

She looked up at him, and was jolted by the glowing tenderness she saw in his eyes, the startling blue seeming to be lit from within by a burning warmth that only last night she had never expected to see again.

Her eyes melted into his. 'Yes, sir! Anything you say, Mr Wild. You're the boss.'

HARLEQUIN

Romance®

Coming Next Month

#3205 FIREWORKS! Ruth Jean Dale
Question: What happens when two blackmailing grandfathers coerce a
dashing rodeo cowboy and his estranged Boston-society wife into spending
time together in Hell's Bells, Texas? Answer: *Fireworks!*

#3206 BREAKING THE ICE Kay Gregory
When hunky Brett Jackson reenters Sarah's life after ten years, he brings a
young son, two dogs and a ferret. His questionable reputation comes, too—
which doesn't make him the kind of guy an ice maiden should melt....

#3207 MAN OF TRUTH Jessica Marchant
Sent to Switzerland to promote a new vacation package, Sally has no idea
she'll have to confront Kemp Whittaker. Film producer, TV presenter, nature
lover and every woman's fantasy, he opposes Sally and everything she stands
for. Can she withstand his assault?

#3208 A KIND OF MAGIC Betty Neels
Fergus Cameron's arrogance makes him the kind of man most women find
annoying, and Rosie is no exception. Admittedly, he can be charming when it
suits him—not that it matters to her. Fergus has already told her he's found
the girl he's going to marry.

#3209 FAR FROM OVER Valerie Parv
Jessie knows that no matter how hard she tries, there's no way to stop
Adrian Cole from coming back into her life. She knows she wants a second
chance with him—but she's afraid of her reaction to her son, Sam.

#3210 BOTH OF THEM Rebecca Winters
Bringing home the wrong baby—it's got to be a one-in-a-billion chance. Yet
Cassie Arnold's sister, Susan, believed it had happened to her. With Susan's
tragic death, Cassie's obliged to continue her sister's investigation. And she
discovers, to her shock, that Susan was right; her real nephew is living with
divorced Phoenix banker Trace Ramsey, as his son. When Trace becomes
aware of the truth, he insists on having *both* children. There's only one
solution, he says—Cassie will have to marry him....
Both of Them is the third title in The Bridal Collection.

AVAILABLE THIS MONTH:

OVER THE YEARS, TELEVISION HAS BROUGHT
THE LIVES AND LOVES OF MANY CHARACTERS INTO
YOUR HOMES. NOW HARLEQUIN INTRODUCES YOU
TO THE TOWN AND PEOPLE OF

One small town—twelve terrific love stories.

GREAT READING...GREAT SAVINGS...
AND A FABULOUS FREE GIFT!

Each book set in Tyler is a self-contained love story; together, the
twelve novels stitch the fabric of the community.

By collecting proofs-of-purchase found in each Tyler book, you can
receive a fabulous gift, ABSOLUTELY FREE! And use our special
Tyler coupons to save on your next TYLER book purchase.

Join us for the fifth TYLER book,
BLAZING STAR by Suzanne Ellison, available in July.

Is there really a murder cover-up?
Will Brick and Karen overcome differences and find true love?